Storylandia

The Wapshott Journal of Fiction

Issue 39

The Wapshott Press

Storylandia, Issue 39, The Wapshott Journal of Fiction, ISSN 1947-5349, ISBN 978-1-942007-39-5 is published at intervals by the Wapshott Press, now a 501(c)(3) nonprofit, PO Box 31513, Los Angeles, California, 90031-0513, telephone 323-201-7147. All correspondence can be sent to The Wapshott Press, PO Box 31513, LA CA 90031-0513. Visit our website at www.WapshottPress.org to learn more.

Storylandia is always seeking quality original short stories, novelettes, and novellas. Please have a look at our submission guidelines at www.Storylandia.WapshottPress.org or email the editor at editor@wapshottpress.org

Donations happily accepted at www.donate.wapshottpress.org

Cover photograph by Scott Pedersen.

"Keep away from People" was originally published in *The Oddville Press*, Spring 2020.

"The Cow Jumped over the Moon" was originally published in *Sobotka Literary Magazine*, 2015.

"Philly is Listening" was originally published in Issue 37/1 of *Louisiana Literature: A Review of Literature and the Humanties*, Southeastern Louisiana University, Hammond, Louisiana, 2020.

Storylandia

The Wapshott Journal of Fiction

Founded in 2009

Issue 39, Autumn 2021

Edited by Ginger Mayerson

Contents

Jerry Cunningham

The Dancing Chameleon

Hoofer and Alma were born on the last night of the last day of the 19th century and were left on the wood steps of Emanuel in a basket covered in a pile of blankets that the pastor, at first, thought was a New Year's present from a parishioner until he heard the high-pitched cries of two hungry babies. No one ever figured out who the momma was so the babies were set to be given to an orphanage up in Danville when Mrs. Chambers sent a messenger on horseback to the pastor with a note requesting his presence for tea. Mrs. Frances Nelson Chambers had been married to Horatio for as long as anyone could remember; his land stretched on to the hills and his cows fattened nicely and he was about to file papers in the courthouse that showed his ownership of all river water and rainwater in the county, along with a plan to rent the water to the sweet-potato farmers along the river banks, when he got angry with Mrs. Chambers at dinner one night in the dining room and choked on a chicken bone and died. Mrs. Chambers wore black for a year, which came as no surprise since she was color blind and had worn black for most of her life. Mrs. Chambers had the rose bushes cut down and replaced with pebbles and closed up the house and lived out of one massive bedroom with scarlet velvet curtains and huge empty vases and a portrait of Horatio holding a fountain pen in the air right next to his shiny, red nose and everyone thought that she would live out her years in bitter widowhood surrounded by rumors of Horatio's massive debts and his decades of punctual visits down to Lulu White's place. So everyone was surprised that Mrs. Chambers desired to raise the twins.

"I can offer those children civilization," Mrs. Chambers told the pastor. "Nothing more and nothing less."

Mrs. Chambers, who always had the look on her face that she had just bitten into a lemon, had it in her head that the Europeans had created a civilization that combined a penchant for respect for one's betters with rich French chowders and sturdy Dutch waffles and the finest sausages of German smokehouses. That civilization, threatened with loss by the nosy American-style addiction to progress and change and other such claptrap, was based, she concluded, on the firm foundation known as the dairymaid. Books covered in leather in Horatio's library had shown Mrs. Chambers unimpeachable evidence that dairymaids were honest, faithful and hardworking, kept good accounts of milk received and cheese and butter made, were capable of taking charge of poultry, and, above all, were modest and blushed easily. If she ever had a daughter, Mrs. Chambers had sworn to her barren husband during formal Sunday dinners, a man who always listened as best he could through the haze of wine and brandy which emanated from the visible pores of his red nose - a gray nose to her, but animated nevertheless - and blazing cheeks, that girl would be a dairymaid, for any girl so delicate that she can place eggs under sitting hens would grow into a fine woman for the finest sons of the finest planters in Virginia. So, Alma grew up wearing Dutch clogs and milking cows and startled by the antics of the little red rooster in the barnyard.

One day at the end of the summer after Hoofer's first encounters with chameleons, Mrs. Chambers stood on the porch and rang the tiny silver bell that she used to summon Alma and sat down with Alma on the swing. It was time, Mrs. Chambers said, for Alma to dress for success, as the boys would be calling on her in no time at all; and though Mrs. Chambers had a closet full of black dresses that could have been hemmed for Alma, Mrs. Chambers lacked the proper shoes for a girl who would soon be noticed by boys with prospects of fine future inheritances, and thus, Mrs. Chambers said, Alma must go to Buford and meet the cobbler and have a pair of black patent shoes made with a little leather bow above the laces.

"Do you promise to follow my instructions to the letter?" asked Mrs. Chambers.

"Of course, Mother," said Alma.

"Keep your eyes peeled for the thin man by the courthouse with the long red hair and one milky eye and trainman's overalls, " Mrs. Chambers said. "They say he carries an ax at night in the woods."

The cobbler measured Alma's feet and gave a wizened look at her clogs and asked her about the color of the patent shoes that she desired.

"My mother told me to get red shoes," she lied.

And so it was that Alma could be seen on her porch humming with her red shoes swinging under her, and her dairy maid duties were lessened so that she could learn to sew and to prepare for school in the fall, and then one day, as she hummed, the red shoes moved in time to the tune of their own volition. Alma danced across the porch with verve. After that, from time to time, the red shoes would break into a dance and smiling Alma hummed and sang and danced and, in an all-around way, enjoyed her liberation from the endless flies and the stench of the cows and their whining every morning as they crowded around the barn, aching to be milked by the exhausted Alma. The schoolhouse was a long, long walk away but Alma danced down the paths, she danced in the sun, she danced in the rain, and she noticed the admiring glances at her shiny shoes by the boys and the jealous stares of the girls. When the teachers were not looking, Alma would show the other kids dance steps that were more fun and faster than the slow, ponderous waltzes of their parents. Alma liked the attention and finished sixth grade with lots of friends and a knack for knitting; Mrs. Chambers, proud of Alma's development despite, Mrs. Chambers repeatedly said, the handicap of that curly hair, never had an inkling that the shoes were red. Mrs. Chambers also overlooked as a teenage whim the fact that Alma would occasionally kick her in the shins under the dining room table.

One day, the pastor came by the house for a rare visit. He sat at the dining room table with Mrs. Chambers and smiled and fussed with a doily and drank tea. Alma came into the dining room wearing a black dress and the pastor exclaimed: "What delightful red shoes, Alma!"

The left eyebrow of Mrs. Chambers arched into a perfect inverted "V"; once the pastor left, the screams of Mrs. Chambers frightened the chickens and caused consternation among the cows.

"You lied! You tricked me! After all I've done for you, you are just an ingrate!" yelled Mrs. Chambers.

Alma's red shoes began to move against her will, and soon Alma was dancing circles around Mrs. Chambers.

"And you mock me, too!" cried Mrs. Chambers. "I should have let you rot in the orphanage!"

Alma wanted to explain, but had no time to do so, for the red shoes began dancing out of the dining room and across the porch and down the path and past the schoolhouse and on towards the woods and the hills and Alma could not stop them. On and on danced poor Alma, exhausted and hot and thirsty, and she entered the woods and amazed the squirrels who watched her from the sides of their eyes and then Alma climbed up the hills, but the red shoes were alive with the sound of their own music. At dusk, she returned to the woods, defeated, as the red shoes slowed their incessant spirited dance to a traditional waltz and finally the red shoes stopped moving and Alma, lost and scared, sat on a log and wept and fell asleep on a bed of pine needles.

Alma awoke in the middle of the night, cold and confused, and she saw an orange moon through the trees, a round, orange, full moon, and she wanted to go home and apologize to her mother; Alma wanted to swear allegiance to black shoes. Then Alma realized that it was no orange moon: it was the round face of the man with the trainman's overalls and he had a red ax and said: "Fine night for a dance!"

Alma ran and ran towards the house, but, as soon as she got close, the red shoes pulled her in the direction of the woods again, and Alma screamed for her brother. Hoofer woke up, dressed quickly and ran after his sister and tackled her before she got to the woods.

"These shoes won't stop dancing!" cried Alma.

Hoofer grabbed the shoes and peeled them off of Alma's feet and held the shoes in his arms as he walked with Alma back home. Hoofer found a large, empty hatbox and put the red shoes in it. For months afterwards, Alma had nightmares and screamed these words in her sleep: "Shine two shoes, shine two shoes!"

Hoofer, at sixteen, had grown tall and lean; he tried to saw wood, but straight cuts turned out all wiggly; he tried to ride a horse, but always fell off; he tried to carry the heavy milk cans, but always ended up playing the drums on them with a stick. Hoofer had two favorite things in life. First, finding chameleons - when they fight with each other, Hoofer noticed, they puff up a funny throat pouch and turn red all over. When they lose a fight they turn brown and give up and hang from the branch upside down. Chameleons turned leaf-green in seconds in the leaves in the summer; in the winter, they were gray with white dots. Hoofer's other favorite thing was listening to Cheeky Jones play the piano on Sundays, and eventually Mr. Jones was nice enough to give Hoofer piano lessons during the week, though Hoofer kept these lessons a secret from his mother. Mr. Jones's stories were all about Chicago - there were jobs there with good money unloading ships on the docks, or delivering coal, or doing kitchen work in the restaurants. You can pick up a tin Christmas horn your first week and save your pennies and then get a trumpet or a banjo for a song from any pawnbroker if you wanna learn to play, he said. You ever wanna make money on the side by playing music, you gotta learn to sight read the music sheet. And you can watch the dance bands for free if you get a job in a nightclub or a dance hall. Later, Mr. Jones said, if you learn to play and the girls are dancing, stick to two beats, not four, and the girls will get up and dance by themselves these days if the fella is flat-footed and glued to his chair.

So, at night in bed, Hoofer dreamt of Chicago and having cash in his pocket and seeing snow and going to bed whenever he felt like it and maybe meeting city girls on trolley cars, but he did not dream of horns or banjos: he dreamt of drums. He dreamt that he was the finest drummer in Chicago, an ace at drumming for toe-dancing: on time when the toes hit the floor and banging that bass drum when the guy caught the girl. Hoofer dreamt of taking a waltz and making it hot; making a long, clean roll on a snare; wearing a bow tie and smoking a small cigar.

And so it was that Hoofer, in his seventeenth year, on a day when the smells of spring were steaming, left a goodbye note for his sister and, with a suitcase in one arm and the hatbox in the other, made his way to Danville and on to Roanoke for a train ride that would end up in Chicago. And it was all true and more: the South Side was noisy and the trolleys and streets were filled with women and girls with aprons and work uniforms and among them were shopgirls and seamstresses and fancy girls with bobbed hair and feather fans and satin coats. Hoofer got a job right away at the docks - heavy work, sweaty work, but he was happy lugging crates and learning the juiciest swear words of each nationality. He bought a snare drum from a pawnbroker and practiced for hours on end in the rooming house; he found himself whistling the newest tunes in the streets and doing splits over fire hydrants. He got a job carrying kegs and bottles and sweeping up at a nightclub. For months and months Hoofer watched the bands bring the men and women to their feet to dance to ragtime and dance

The Black Bottom and *The Argentine Tango*. Men paid for dance partners and bottle parties got out of hand and fights broke out like clockwork and one night, after work, while smoking a short cigar in the alley, an old song and dance man was getting mellow on a bottle of cheap whiskey and the man told Hoofer about the newfangled thing on dance shoes for men: taps.

"I've got these taps on my hard old buck and wing shoes," the man said, "but I've got a secret: I bought a pair of soft shoes and now I can tap like a snare drum and I've got a secret that is mine, and mine alone, 'til I die."

"What's your secret?" asked Hoofer. "It's safe with me."

"My secret," said the man after a healthy chug on the bottle, "is that I toss sand onto the bandstand or the dance floor, and I tap with my soft shoes, and I sound like one of those drummers with those fancy brush sticks."

For the next year, Hoofer worked and saved his money and watched the musicians play at lawn parties, at parties in the park, and at the tonks, where the dockworkers and stonemasons and doormen and telegraph messengers mixed with the dancing girls and the men drank corn-liquor and covered up the holes in the pool table so they could play craps. Soon, soldiers on crutches came back from the war and then all the men came back and the women drank Pink Ladies in the tonks and, later still, at the more upscale dance halls and music halls, the young women with brown trousers and fake pearl necklaces and ivory bangles and French berets and smart eyes danced *The Foxtrot* at high speed with high kicks, accompanied by slow men. Dance competitions were held wherever there was a ball: at each Victory In Europe Ball, the musicians were not only paid, but they were given fancy dinners of rooster combs and sweet potatoes and midnight snacks of deviled ham on biscuits. Chorus girls began to notice Hoofer, who looked sharp on his nights off with a three-piece suit and two-tone shoes. *The Foxtrot* was said by medical doctors to cure women of stammering and, combined with two packs of cigarettes a day, to keep a woman's weight down. From time to time the newspapers carried headlines of an important minister preaching against the depravity of *The Foxtrot* and the moral threat posed by *The Bunny Hug*. Local citizens, true and good, dedicated their energies to stamping out freak steps throughout Chicago, from the high schools to the speakeasies. Tango Balls were held for a year, but faded because the male customers were scared off by the speed and dexterity required; things picked up when Blues Balls came around, and the Chicago dance scene spiked with the conquest of *The Charleston. The Charleston* resulted in well-attended competitions and eventually there were signs in the dancehalls that said "P.C.Q." (Please Charleston Quietly). With its violent side-kicks and, in the minds of the gentry, its freak steps and sinful nature, along with, in the minds of the doctors, its ability to damage the ankles of slender young women, *The Charleston* too attracted opposition; but girls from the suburbs began to sneak out of their homes at night to the dance halls and pretty dress competitions sprouted all over after midnight. Of course there were still fights by jealous males wherever there was music and women and drink, though the most memorable gang fights were the product of the seething hatreds between the Freudian men of German descent and the Dadaists of

French descent.

Through these years Hoofer, at the rooming house, practiced tap dancing on the hardwood floors, and the other boarders smiled, as did the landlady, for Hoofer had talent. The snare drum gathered dust. One day, walking down the street, Hoofer saw a construction sign blown over by the cold winds off of Lake Michigan and the sign lay on the sidewalk: he jumped on it and danced with his tap shoes on, and a crowd formed of admirers. From then on, Hoofer became a street corner tap dancer with a homemade tap mat of plywood, and the street dancing paid remarkably well, so he upgraded his wardrobe to include a bowler hat and a cane with a lion's head and he ended up teaching tap dance at an upscale dance studio for excellent money. By the age of thirty, Hoofer had - along with the hatbox - a radio, a record player, a collection of records that he ordered from mail catalogues, a collection of his beloved sheet music, white carnations in the lapels of his five double-breasted suits, boisterous cufflinks, soft tap shoes colored gold or blue or red depending on his mood, hard black tap shoes that he shined with polish every day and buffed with a soft cloth, a cologne from France that was guaranteed "to make the ladies faint," and offers from the cabarets and the fancified dance halls to perform acts on stage. Hoofer, in his early thirties, sporting a thin mustache and an easy smile, played a clown, played a policeman, played a man with a harem, and played a railroad conductor who broke into a dance called *The Chattanooga Choo Choo*. By his mid-thirties, tap dance had gone mainstream, and Hoofer sent regular cashier's checks back home to Virginia, to which he only returned once, to his mother's funeral, which he later remembered only for the fact that the snare drummer in the Dixieland band that Hoofer hired to follow her coffin to the cemetery had put a red and white spotted handkerchief under the snares of his drum to deaden the sound. Hoofer thought it was a nice touch.

On the night of his thirty-fifth birthday, New Year's Eve, Hoofer had bought his first-ever bottle of champagne at a fancy dance club that sported a crystal chandelier. Then, a young woman with a thin waist and a pretty skirt and shapely eyebrows and a gray squirrel coat and coffee skin and snakeskin shoes walked into the club. Hoofer offered to buy her a drink and when she said, sure, how about an Orange Blossom, her deep, melty voice made him suddenly realize why men get married. Her name was Chartreuse, her eyes were green and, after one drink, Hoofer asked her what the name of her perfume. When Chartreuse replied that she wasn't wearing any perfume, Hoofer realized why men stay married. Before the night was over, Hoofer and Chartreuse were laughing and completely at ease with each other.

At four in the morning, Chartreuse said: "Hoofer, be a good man and walk me home. And then you are taking off, no funny business. After all, I've got a derringer in my garter!"

Hoofer laughed hard and, in his heart, swore eternal devotion.

Hoofer created dances just for Chartreuse; when they were alone, he performed them for her, with feeling.

Hoofer wrote Alma a letter that gushed with romantic descriptions of Chartreuse, describing her as a "shapely dish." Hoofer closed the letter this way: "She makes the rest of the girls look like bologna sausages!"

Love blossomed, as did Hoofer's career. Chicago sported dozens of tap studios; children were now safe in dance halls; teaching gigs were plentiful for Hoofer. The first gray hairs on his temples did not slow him down: in fact, Hoofer became known for his aggressive version of *The Lindy Hop*. One night, after performing *The Lindy Hop* before a sit-down audience in a theatre and backed by a swing orchestra, the master of ceremonies was tackled on stage by a radical preacher. The preacher declared into the microphone that the dance was "devilish" and that the music was "bringing us down to the level of minstrels with bongos and motor horns and tin plates."

The next day, Hoofer got in touch with a real estate agent and wrote out a ten-year plan for his career and his impending marriage. Within a month, the newly-married Hoofer and Chartreuse moved into their first home: an older, two-bedroom home with a bathtub with lion's feet and a basement with a workbench. Hoofer had a walk-in closet for his double-breasted suits and the hatbox had a prominent place on a top shelf.

Just after moving into his new home, Hoofer went to three Greek delicatessens and bought up all of their goat's milk; night after night, for the rest of his life, he bathed in yellow lemon juice and white goat's milk.

Hoofer's fortieth year found him entertaining troops for the USO all around Army bases in the U.S. and, now married to Chartreuse, the father of a son named Phil. One night during a gig at Mama Dinks, while spreading sand on the bandstand in preparation for an act featuring a toned-down version of *The Jitterbug*, a drunken sailor showed Hoofer his American flag tattoo on his right arm.

"You oughtta get one," said the sailor. "It'll show on you."

The following week found Hoofer at his workbench surrounded by white glue and a glue gun and lace and sheet music and rhinestones. He decorated a fine pair of dance shoes with sheet music and, once the glue had dried for the rhinestones, festooned the top and the back with red, white and blue feathers. These dance shoes became Hoofer's trademark as he toured with the USO to Alaska, Paris and finally to a military base in British Guiana, where Hoofer contracted for his first movie and contracted malaria; he died shortly afterwards in a Chicago hospital.

Phil inherited the hatbox, grew up to become a podiatrist and married in his twenties. Phil had a son - born during the early 70's - named Buck, who became a moody boy with no apparent skills and notable only for his smelly feet and his collection of mood rings. Mood rings were a 70's craze: they were plastic rings that changed colors with the wearer's moods.

Phil, a fastidious man with a passion for toe manicures, was in a cleaning frenzy one weekend and tossed the hatbox in the trash - the red shoes, dimmed to dull brown and lacking polish for decades, were, Phil felt, a lost cause. Buck, who had grown up hearing stories about his grandfather's cheery career as a Chicago tap dancer, snuck out to the trash can and rescued the hatbox; Buck hid it at the bottom of his bedroom closet. Buck got ahold of red shoe polish and polished the red shoes and placed them in the hatbox. Phil's cleaning frenzy had not abated by the following week when he came across Buck's stinking ratty sneakers in the living room: they were then dumped by Phil in the trash can. Buck rescued the ratty sneakers and secreted them into the hatbox with the red shoes.

Hours later, in his bedroom, Buck heard a voice from his closet.

"Get me out of here!" cried the voice. "It stinks in here!"

Buck opened the closet door and saw black smoke rising from the edges of the hat box. Buck opened the cover to the hatbox and black smoke billowed out, twisting and growing in the middle of the bedroom. A genii appeared with a turban.

"I can't tell you how advantageous a little baby powder on your feet at night will be for you, my son," said the genii. "Also, it's my destiny to tell you that if you shine both red shoes - if you shine two shoes at once - you then get one wish."

Buck did so.

"What would you like the most in the world?" asked the genii. "You get one wish: make it a good one, my son."

At that moment, Buck thought of his dancing grandfather and of the legend of the dance shoes with the red, white and blue feathers, and Buck, after returning the red shoes to the hatbox, made the first firm decision of his life.

"I want a new pair of bouncy sneakers covered with mood rings!" Buck cried. "And also covered with red, white and blue feathers!"

The left eyebrow of the genii arched into a perfect inverted "V" and a new pair of sneakers covered with mood rings and feathers appeared. The genii disappeared.

Buck enjoyed showing his friends the fact that the new sneakers turned red when he was angry and blue when he was sad and green when he was jealous.

But, within a year, the new sneakers looked soggy, the feathers were beginning to bald, and the rubber soles had lost their bounce. The skills of the mood rings became unhinged and now they reflected the moods of neighborhood cats and basement insects. Buck opened up the hatbox with the red shoes and the smelly sneakers inside and tossed in the new sneakers that were covered with feathers and mood rings; the saddened mood rings on the sneakers promptly turned blue.

One day, during a cleaning frenzy, Phil desired to clean out the basement; he saw an ad in the newspaper that said: "Man With A Truck. Will Collect Trash And Refuse And Bring To County Dump. No Job Too Small." That day, Phil examined Buck's closet.

A rickety old pickup truck with wood panels slowly squealed to a halt in front of the house; out came two young men who began to take shovels off of the side of the truck; a skinny old man, with faded red hairs sticking out from the back of his baseball cap and a milky eye, got out slowly from the driver's side. Later, at the smelly edge of the county dump, the young men shoveled refuse off of the back of the truck. Flying through the air sailed a pair of ratty sneakers and a pair of red shoes and a newish pair of blue sneakers with feathers: the blue sneakers seemed to spin and dance, with feeling.

Scott Pedersen

Philly Is Listening!

Welcome to "Philly Is Listening!" I'm your host, Skip Lusky, and I thank you for once again inviting us into your home. Unlike drama programs at other radio stations, we bring you family drama as it happens, on location, and, as always, unrehearsed. Yes, there's a reason why last year we were voted the most popular radio drama program of 1937 in greater Philadelphia. Our producer today is Peter Rasmussen, and our sponsor, as always: the fine people at Mitchelson Shaving Products. "We're cutting it close!"

Today, we'll be witnessing a lunchtime encounter between Bert, a retired gentleman whose well-to-do sister has recently passed away, and his niece, Lois. Now, our research has found that Bert is the executor of his sister's estate—so keep that in mind—and her will has given everything to Lois. But here's the fly in the ointment: the original will can't be found. There's just the carbon copy in Lois's possession. These inheritance situations can be a real tinderbox, ladies and gentlemen. Let's see what flares up between these two over lunch.

There's Bert, already seated at a round table all laid out with a fine linen tablecloth, polished water goblets, crisp cloth napkins folded into flower shapes—let me tell you, this is one classy establishment, no run-of-the-mill steakhouse. It was selected by Lois, although Bert is treating today. Peter, do you think Bert looks a little like Jimmy Cagney? Yes, you're right, more like Jimmy Cagney's father. Not really like the lithe movie star himself.

Bert is dressed casually. Comfortably, I would say. He sure looks comfortable settled into that red leather arm chair. I wish my chair could compare, but I'm not complaining. I'm here in our sound-proof booth, which was checked earlier today to ensure that Bert and Lois can't hear me. But trust me, I can see and hear everything.

And here comes Lois. She's just entered the restaurant and is all decked out in a fitted hounds-tooth jacket. She's looking around, and now she sees Bert. She walks over to the table and sits across from him. I noticed he didn't get up. Yes, Peter, it could be hard for him.

And now Bert has raised his oxblood-colored menu. You should see this menu, with the gold loop and tassel, and there's the steakhouse name embossed in gold on the front: "Stephan's Prime."

This is going to be a tough choice. By the way, we'd like to thank Stephan's for the wonderful breakfasts this morning, and all we had to do was sign a waiver regarding today's program—just to keep them off the hook legally in case things go awry. Yes, friends, it's that kind of attention to detail that has kept Stephan's in business all these years.

Peter tells me we've just switched on our hidden microphone, so let's listen in as Bert makes his selection.

"Look at these fucking prices!"

I have to apologize, ladies and gentlemen. That was Bert. I hadn't figured him for an egg. Research can do only so much. That's one of the risks of live radio, but well worth it, I can assure you, and with any luck we'll be back with another edition of the program next week. We appreciate your sticking with us. Now, let's get back to the action.

Bert has lowered his menu. "What kind of restaurant did you pick? I'm not made of money, you know."

Lois looks perturbed. "You wanted steak, Uncle Bert. It's very good here."

"It better be."

"Look around. Aren't these people enjoying theirs?"

Bert is looking around the room. "Bunch of goddamn doctors. Driving up prices."

Once again, I apologize. We're going to take a break right now so you can hear about some fine Mitchelson products and listen to some sweet dance music while Bert and Lois enjoy their meal.

Welcome back to the action, ladies and gentlemen. If I sound a little rattled—well, I'll explain later. For those of you who are listening to the program for the first time or have certain moral reservations, think of it as listening in on a party line. When you pick up your telephone receiver at home, you never know what you're going to hear. It's just part of modern life.

Well, Bert and Lois have finished dining on some of the best-looking Porterhouse steaks I've ever seen, and their table has been cleared of dishes. It seems they may now be getting down to brass tacks.

I can see that Bert has pulled out some kind of document. "That lawyer you recommended wants another two hundred for his fee, but he said he'll settle for half that if I can show the estate's funds are depleted. That's where you come in."

Bert has tossed the document onto the table, followed by a pen. "Sign the last page."

Lois has picked up the document and is flipping through it. Now she's looking up at Bert. She seems pretty unhappy about something. "I can't sign this. It says I received a thousand dollars more than I did."

"Don't worry about it. He'll never know. Just sign. I want to wrap this up."

Oh, my. I think Bert is going to need a different kind of lawyer. With this live broadcast, the cat's really out of the bag now.

Lois is shaking her head. "You're asking me to help you defraud a lawyer—who happens to be a friend of mine—over a hundred dollars."

"Do you know how much lawyers make? You barely know him. Who the hell cares?"

"Legal expenses should come out of the estate. I'll give you some money back to cover it."

Did you hear that? Bert has just pounded the table with his fist. "My sister wanted you to have all that money!"

"Bert, I'm really grateful. You've put in a lot of time and effort. And it must have been painful for you."

Bert has lowered his head. I would call his expression...forlorn. "My sister practically raised your dad and me."

"I didn't know that. Dad never said much about you or Aunt Candice."

"Especially me, I bet. Too embarrassing for him. Well, let me fill you in." Bert is leaning back in his chair now. "Instead of a bladder, I've got a bag of piss strapped to my leg. Next month they have to go back in and fix my hip again. It's killin' me."

Once again, I apologize, ladies and gentlemen. This usually doesn't happen. What's that, Peter? Peter has reminded me of our program last April with the drill sergeant. Thank you, Peter. You know, we couldn't put on a program like this without our crackerjack staff.

Wait, it looks like Bert is wincing. He's really laying it on like gangbusters. Lois looks concerned. And now Bert has leaned forward again. "Making sure your aunt's final wishes are followed will give me some pleasure. And I don't care if somebody doesn't like how I go about it."

I think he may be getting to Lois. Yes, Lois is softening. I can see it in her face, even from here. "Bert, when I came to help Aunt Candice move last year, you had everything already packed. You did that while you were in pain?"

"Hell, if you're dedicated to somebody, you ignore pain—and your scruples, Miss Goody Two-Shoes—to do that one thing they really need."

"Uncle Bert, you don't have to do this for me. My copy of the will has no legal weight. Legally, as next of kin, you're entitled to the estate."

"Who cares what the law says?" Bert is motioning around the room now. "Besides you, who the hell cares?"

Lois is looking over at the corner of the room. A man is getting up from a table there. A good-looking man, and that's quite a suit he's wearing. That couldn't be off-the-rack, could it, Peter? I think Lois recognizes him. Yes, she's given him a little wave. "He cares."

Now the man is walking over to Bert and Lois's

table. "Hello, Lois. Hello, Bert." Judging from her smile, I'd say Lois likes this fellow.

Bert has a funny expression on this face—I would call it unfriendly. Now he's looking the man up and down. "Well, there he is. The highway robber himself."

Listen to the man laugh. It sounds phony to me. Does it to you? "Bert, I've really enjoyed working with you. Never a dull moment. What's that? It looks like the form I sent you."

The man has picked up the document and is flipping through it. "It's all filled out. Just needs a signature. I can take it with me and save you the postage."

My goodness, look at Bert glare at Lois. That stare would wilt an oak tree, ladies and gentlemen. "As if I didn't have enough grief, my niece here won't sign."

Now the man is staring at Lois as well. We have two highly dissatisfied men in this picture, believe you me.

Lois looks flummoxed. Yes, she's in a real pickle. She sure can't tell the lawyer about Bert's scheme, but then why isn't she signing? You get the picture. Our Lois looks like a soft touch, the kind of woman who would want to help out her uncle, especially after that sob story. But cheat her lawyer friend? Not her style. So, what is she going to do? So far, she's speechless.

And now the lawyer has put the document back on the table. "Just drop it in the mail when you get a chance." No time-wasting for this guy. They say time is money for a lawyer. Ain't that the truth! And there he goes, walking away. I would describe his expression as smug.

Ooh, Bert is wincing again. I'm starting to feel

some hip pain myself just looking at him. Peter, can we ask the waiter to bring Bert an aspirin or something? What? You're right, we shouldn't interfere. This isn't the time to stick our noses into Bert's business.

Now Lois is looking at the document. This young woman is deep in thought, the picture of pensive, to coin a phrase. This lull in the action is all due to a dilemma being faced by our ethical friend Lois. Don't think I'm just bumping gums here, but allow me to speculate as to her train of thought. She's thinking, what would be the harm? After all, the lawyer would never know, and this is something Bert really needs.

She's picked up the pen! Lois is holding the pen over the document, as if she's about to sign. Did you hear Bert's chair creak just now? Bert is really leaning into that table. Lois must be feeling tremendous pressure to sign right now. Our microphone is picking up Bert's heavy breathing. Just imagine what Lois is experiencing as the seconds tick by.

It looks like Bert has something to say. His eyes are bulging a bit. "While we're still young!"

Well, I don't know if that's going to be effective for Bert. And just when he had sympathy on his side.

Now Lois is looking over at the cash register. The lawyer is paying for his meal. My goodness, look at that roll! This fellow is loaded to the gills. I wonder if seeing that wad of cash is going to sway Lois toward signing. I wouldn't bet on it, though. Our Lois strikes me as the honest type who wouldn't cross anyone, not even a wealthy lawyer. I think she's going to do right by him.

And there it is! Lois has dropped the pen onto the table. "I'm sorry, Uncle Bert. It was very decent of him to offer to reduce his bill. Let's not take advantage.

It wouldn't be fair."

"After I poured my goddamn heart out?"

"I have to go. Thank you for lunch. When the form is fixed, I'll sign it. But, uh, mail it to me. Let's not meet for a meal."

Lois has gotten up and is heading for the door. Well, ladies and gentlemen, Bert had high hopes for this lunch, but it's turned out to be a real trip for biscuits for him. Now he's turned to the people at the next table. I suppose he's feeling pretty crushed right about now and needs to talk to someone, anyone. "Can you believe these prices? Sixteen dollars for two goddamn steaks. And my niece didn't even finish hers!"

I hate to sound like a broken record, ladies and gentlemen, but I do apologize for any discomfort you may have experienced during today's program. I feel I know our audience, and what a supportive group you all are. And we're certainly sorry to see the folks at Mitchelson Shaving Products bid us adieu.

What's that, Peter? Yes, it's time for the tag. Peter is a real eager beaver today. I don't know what's gotten into him. Now he's showing me Phillies tickets. And I thought *Bert* was loyal. Well, we don't want to keep the team waiting. They might score a run today. So, be sure to join us next week, with a new sponsor and the always-helpful—and hopeful—Peter Rasmussen. Until then, watch what you say—Philly is listening!

William Cass

The Cow Jumped Over the Moon

As I sit here now, watching the snow silently fall, and think about events in isolation, they do seem strange. But when things took place, when they were slowly tumbling over themselves, they made sense. And with the accumulation of passing time, I'm content that they worked out as they should have. I might even say as they had to.

I'd just celebrated my fifty-eighth birthday by selling my graphics arts business in Seattle to a competitor across town. With what I got from selling the business and my house, I was able to buy a little condo near the tree line outside of Santa Fe. I hadn't been to the area since 1976 almost four decades earlier when I'd done community organizing there after college. It was where I met my ex-wife, so maybe it reminded me of happier times. I found the condo when I'd been in Albuquerque for a work convention and had driven over out of nostalgia, I guess. I bought it on the spur of the moment. I'd grown tired of the rain and had thought from time to time about relocating. It had been ten years since my ex-wife's affair and our divorce, and twelve since she'd moved down to Portland with her new husband. I'd thought at the time that our son would stay with me and finish high school, but he'd chosen to go with her. Then four years later, he'd died in a ski accident. Each event had jarred something inside of me and contributed to my sudden decision to sell and move.

Nick Phillips was a longtime client, but I can't say I knew him well. On a kind of whim, he'd started his fishing lodge on a little island about four hundred miles up the British Columbian coast from Vancouver. He and his wife had run a successful counseling business in Olympia and he told me he got tired of dealing with other people's problems day in and day out. He said he just asked himself one sleepless night how he could make a living doing something he loved and the fishing idea put itself together.

He looked around and found that remote spot advertised on the internet. It had begun as a Finnish potato farm, had later become a kind of hippie commune, and had finally sat empty for a number of years. His plan was to create a combination fishing and first-class dining/lodging experience largely designed for corporate outings of several days at a time. He thought that equation would lend itself to a steady stream of primarily repeat customers who could foot an expensive bill without blinking. His idea worked well.

The place started as a group of old buildings on a hill above the water. He turned the main farmhouse into a dining area with some anterooms for relaxing and recreation, built a cluster of small log cabins that were rustic but well-appointed, repaired an old stone and mortar sauna, added a couple of hot tubs and decks, bought a few secondhand boats set-up for fishing, fixed the dock, hired a few locals as guides and college kids from down south on summer break for staff, found a chef from San Francisco for the season, and opened for business. He had some established contacts to get started, and things went pretty much as he imagined from there. He'd added a new wrinkle here and there and had filled thirty or so trips a year for groups of up to fifteen from late May to mid-September ever since. I did his advertising and had a pretty good idea of his finances; I figured that after expenses, he cleared better than a couple hundred thousand a season.

Nick was a big one for working trades for business. He exchanged all his wine and liquor for portions of trips and did the same thing to reduce costs with the floatplane company he used out of Seattle. He'd been trying to swing a deal with me for years. Finally, shortly before I sold out, I agreed to do some last-minute changes on his brochure after it had already been sent to press on the promise of a fishing trip at his lodge anytime I wanted. The truth was I'd spent a couple of summers many years before working on commercial fishing boats in Alaska to help pay for college; I'd pretty much caught all the fish I was interested in for a lifetime.

I'd forgotten about our deal entirely until the morning after the movers had left with my stuff to Santa Fe. I was sleeping on the couch in my office; it was the only thing there except my desk and chair. My cell phone range before I was awake; it was Nick.

"Listen, buddy," he said. "I've got a couple of open spots on my last trip of the season and I want you to come up on that freebie. Quick three-day. We're killing the chinooks right now."

I said, "Nick, I'm leaving for Santa Fe tomorrow.

Movers will be there Saturday."

"Perfect. You help them pile those boxes in your new living room, then get your ass on a plane back to Seattle and be standing tall on the float dock Tuesday afternoon at two. Hell, I'll pay for your flight; my account's still outstanding, isn't it? Bill me."

"Jesus, Nick," I said. However, the idea wasn't without some appeal. Over the last several days, I'd felt a strange loneliness about the move and starting over in New Mexico. I looked out my office window where the familiar layer of heavy-bellied, low clouds drifted over the city.

Nick said, "We've been working together a lot of years, partner. You don't jump on this, we may lose touch, you might never come. What the hell you got waiting for you down there that's so urgent?"

I said, "I guess nothing."

"You're damn right. I'll see you on Tuesday, then. I'll be sure they have a drink waiting for you in Seattle. Send me that bill."

So, I arranged things quickly in Santa Fe and found myself on Tuesday afternoon in a little office off the floatplane hangar in Renton next to Boeing Field. I was waiting with about ten employees of a Midwest beer distributorship, a few of their top clients, and a surgeon from Medina. The beer folks were all drinking cocktails from plastic cups and laughing together near the counter. I stood off a ways trying to make conversation with the surgeon, a stern, well-dressed man who was going along comp, too, in exchange for shearing the alpacas that were Nick's newest addition to the lodge. He told me he'd grown up on a sheep farm in New Zealand, though I could detect no accent. Apparently, he'd gotten to know Nick after doing some repairs on his shoulder.

For all I knew, Nick might have been paying off part of a medical bill, as well; I wouldn't have put it past him.

Three hours later, we were all climbing out of floatplanes onto the Phillips Lodge dock in late afternoon sunshine where Nick and a pretty college-aged girl waited to greet us with a tray of little warm, moistened towels for our faces and necks.

When I stepped onto the dock, Nick gave me one of his customary claps on the shoulder and growled, "Christ, I'm glad you made it. About damn time. This is great." Then he moved on to his paying guests.

I looked over the vista I'd seen many times before on his brochure. The lodge and surrounding cabins sat forty or so yards up the sloping grassy hillside that was dotted with oak and pine trees. Dense spruce forest stood behind it. A wide garden of raised beds in front of the lodge held vegetables and flowers: splashes of color against the green and weathered gray wood. A small corral enclosed by a new split rail fence ran along one side of the property in which several alpacas grazed on the grass; it led to an open barn and some outbuildings that looked like they'd been retrofitted into staff quarters. A scattering of old farm equipment had been left to rust for effect and had grown over here and there with ivy.

A couple of smiling young men dressed in jeans and lodge sweatshirts, who we would later get to know as fishing guides, begun shuttling our bags to the cabins. We followed the hostess past potted geraniums on the sides of the dock up the hill to the wide deck that surrounded the lodge. Nick caught up to me on the way and gave me another squeeze on the shoulder. He told me he looked forward to seeing me but knew I'd understand that he had to spend most of his time with his customers. I told him not to worry and that I appreciated his hospitality. Looking at him, I thought that he'd aged better than I had.

Nick gathered us together on the deck while one of the college girls passed out flumes of champagne from another tray. He welcomed us with a rousing toast to a good catch and then went on to explain which cabins we'd been assigned to, a little about the lodge, the surrounding area, and our trip's itinerary. He told us the immediate plan was to socialize a bit, get unpacked, and then return for dinner at seven.

After I finished the champagne, I went and settled in at my cabin. It was top-notch inside. From its window, I could see Nick and a couple of guides readying the fishing boats at the dock for the morning. Their movements and expressions had a punctuation to them that seemed to border on practiced choreography.

Shortly after seven, I was seated at a large round table in the lodge's dining room with the others. Nick gave us the weather and fishing report for the next morning and told us they'd be providing us with wake-up calls at 5:00AM. Next, he had the college girls hold up the bottles of white and red wine that were going to be served with dinner and gave a description of each. Finally, he led us in hearty applause as he introduced the chef who came bounding up the stairs to explain each course for the night's fare. It was about then that I realized that fishing was not necessarily the primary ingredient in the trip's experience, but that Nick intended pleasant and memorable moments for the guests regardless of how successful the sport might be. It seemed to me on his part both contrived and inspired.

After dinner, most of the party moved into the adjacent game room for billiards, cigars, and cognac. I walked down the hill to the shore. The tide was out, the beach full of kelp and large, barnacle-encrusted rocks. The water moving among them made the sound of children's blocks knocking together. The sky was stained purple over the mountains and black above, full of stars. I looked at things and thought about my life, the part behind me and the one ahead. I watched the red traveling light of a boat out in the channel heading toward Port McNeil. I looked up at the sky and hoped it might turn cold enough for the Northern Lights, though I thought it unlikely. I hadn't seen them since I'd been in Alaska. A few minutes later, I turned and headed up to bed.

That next morning just before full dawn, we were trolling slowly along the shoreline of an area known as Mitchell Bay, four of us to a boat, everyone wearing a poncho and ball cap with the lodge's name and logo. A guide on each boat worked the tiller and tended the lines and outriggers. The early morning's air was cool and damp. As the mountains to the west on Vancouver Island emerged in the muffled light, big heavy-bellied clouds hung against them.

I was on an open boat with the surgeon and two area managers from the distributorship. The three of them sat drinking coffee together on the bow seats up front while I leaned against the stern with the guide. We motored almost imperceptibly about two hundred feet from a long narrow shore of crushed rock and driftwood; the other boats had moved off in their own directions. Strands of straight pines behind the beach led up the hillside towards the top of the island. Except for the soft burbling of the trolling outboard and the mumble of voices from the front of the boat, it was quiet, still.

Our guide's name was Jim. I didn't remember seeing him the evening before. I figured him for about my age. Like me, he had moist, weary eyes, a stubble beard, and was a little bent. His cap was the only one on the boat not advertising the lodge and sat crooked and worn on his head. He wore faded jeans, an old plaid flannel shirt under the open poncho, and high black rubber boots. He kept a cigarette lit most of the time.

"So," he said to me. "You're Nick's advertising man."

I told him all I did was design his brochures. We bobbed along for a while watching the lines. I asked him how long he'd been on the island.

In his quiet voice he told me, "Pretty near forty years now. I did some commercial fishing up on the outside for a while."

"You from here?"

He looked at me evenly for a moment. His eyes were blue-green like mine and crinkled a bit at the edges. He said, "No."

"Been guiding for Nick long?"

He nodded. "Since he started. What's that, seventeen years, I guess? Got tired of fishing for myself. Pretty much phasing out of guiding now, too. Only go out anymore when he's short. I'm his handyman mostly, and caretaker after the season."

"What's involved with that?"

"Not a hell of a lot." He laughed. "Now with the new alpacas, there'll be a little something, I guess." He stopped, studied the tip of one pole, then jumped to it. He pulled it from its harness, jerking in one motion, and shouted, "Fish on! Get those other lines up!"

We all scrambled into the drill Jim had rehearsed with us before leaving. We'd drawn numbers and the surgeon had the first fish, so the rest of us got the other lines out of the way and huddled off to watch him bring it in. Jim stood next to him and said things like, "Perfect...keep the tip up...easy...let it run."

With the way Jim had set the hook and the first long deep dive of the fish, I was pretty sure the surgeon could do just about anything and not lose it. The beer guys cheered him on, and as I watched him grunting in his pressed jeans and alligator boots, I decided that I'd forget how ludicrous the whole thing was and just try to enjoy myself.

After a bit, Jim was able to net the surgeon's salmon and lift it into the boat. We all whooped and hollered while the surgeon beamed. Jim took his picture holding the fish with the surgeon's cell phone.

The tide had already turned and none of us caught anything more that morning. We headed back to the lodge for lunch. All the boats arrived at the dock at about the same time. Nick met us there and led us in a fish weighing ceremony. Seven fish in total had been caught. We all clapped for the biggest fish, which turned out to be the surgeon's.

After lunch, most of the group headed back out on the boats to deeper water to try jigging for halibut and bottom fish. A couple returned to their cabins to rest; a few headed to the sauna and hot tubs. I changed into my own heartier poncho and went for a walk. I wandered along a path through the back of the property and came out on a gravel road that followed the coastline to the north along a bluff. It had begun to rain very lightly. Aside from the forest, the only things I passed were a couple of abandoned spots that looked like they were once small attempts at farming.

One building had an undulating roofline that seemed like it had been built that way intentionally; a rusted iron half-moon with a cow leaping over it was nailed above the door. The road was empty and I thought that perhaps it circled the island. The only sound was of the water in the channel, the soft fall of the rain, and my footsteps in the gravel.

I turned around after a half-hour or so and retraced my steps. I came back on the far side of Nick's property and entered through a gate near the open barn. Jim was inside spreading hay into a narrow feeding trough while the alpacas pranced in the small dirt area next to it. He glanced up as I came over and said hello. He was wearing the same outfit minus the poncho and a cigarette was clenched between his lips. I watched him finish filling the trough, then step away and click to the alpacas. The animals followed one another to the trough, three cream-colored and one brown whose fur was so thick it looked like a saddle around its middle. The brown butted one of the others out of the way and began eating in its place. Chewing, it craned its neck, looked at us, then dipped for more hay.

Jim laughed and said, "You don't want to mess with her. She's testy."

I asked, "The brown?"

He nodded.

"Why are they here anyway?"

Jim cocked his head. "You know Nick. Always working an angle. Course, the guests like the curiosity, and the fur will bring three, four hundred bucks each. But Nick's mostly interested in the money they can generate breeding. A healthy yearling goes for about fifteen grand."

I whistled and said, "No kidding."

Jim nodded again. "The brown's due to give birth in the spring. That'll be our first."

"Where'd you learn to care for them?"

Jim shrugged. "Not much to it, really. Been reading a book. Worked on a farm or two back when." He scratched the brown's head as she ate, the fur there dusty and flaked with bits of straw. He said, "I've always liked animals."

The light in the barn was dim. I heard the distant sound of a motor and turned to see the first of the lodge's boats returning from around the headland.

Dinner that night was a little later than the evening before. While the salad was being served, I looked out the big picture windows across the channel. There was no sunset, though the rain had stopped and the ceiling of clouds had lifted a bit. Nick came over and stood next to my chair to talk for a while. He asked after my family. Our past business relationship had never given him any reason to know about my divorce or the death of my son. I described both briefly. He commiserated, then told me a little about some tribulations with his own marriage and a new business venture he and his wife were trying to start outside of Tucson. The concept was essentially a winter equivalent to the lodge except it was built on a southwestern theme and would cater to trail rides and customized golf packages.

By the time dinner ended, it was nearly full dark. Most of the guests headed into the little nearby village to the local tavern. Nick went off to his house at the back of the property with his two yellow labs. I walked back to my cabin and stood a while against the porch railing. I watched the lights at Nick's house blink off one by one. The tide was going out again, and across the channel I could see the glow of Port McNeil like a rudely tossed string of Christmas lights in the distance. Other than that, it was nothing but water, trees, and mountains in all directions. Lovely.

Down at the entrance to the barn, I saw Jim brushing the back of the big brown alpaca. I watched the curling wisp of smoke from his cigarette and listened to the slow, course pull of the brush. I took my wallet out and looked at the photo of my son, ran my thumb over it. Then I went inside and called it a night.

The next morning, we motored north along the island's curving coastline for better than an hour before putting in. I got my fish not twenty minutes after the lines had been in the water: a small late-season king, skinny but long. I guessed fourteen or fifteen pounds. Our guide was named Geoff, a tall lanky kid with bad teeth and kind eyes. It was just after sunrise and the tide had begun to turn. The sun hadn't yet peeked over the mountains on the mainland, but it promised to be a nice day.

Geoff told me he'd lived on the island since he was three. He helped his dad and uncle at their gas station in the village during the off-season. I asked him what it was like to grow up there and he shrugged.

"All right, I guess. I liked it. Suppose it gets kind of slow for some kids."

"Did hippies really used to live on Nick's property?"

"So the story goes. That was before my time. Ask Jim. He was around then."

A little before noon, we brought in the lines and motored around to a small cove where lunch had been set up for us on the beach. The scene looked a little like a reception area for a fancy outdoor wedding. A canopy had been raised over folding tables and chairs and chamber music was playing from a boom box. The chef was lifting live crabs into a big iron pot suspended over a smoldering fire dug into the sand, and the college girls were seating people and pouring white wine. Nick shuttled folks from the anchored fishing boats to the shore in a dinghy with a small outboard that looked brand new.

We were the last boat in. I could see the surgeon waiting in the back of a skiff with no fishing gear, and I assumed it was what Nick had motored out in himself. When he came for us, I asked Nick about it, and he said he was taking the surgeon back to do the shearing. I asked if I could go with them.

"Suit yourself," Nick said. "But you'll miss this spread. All we have is sandwiches and sodas in a cooler on board."

I told him that was fine. On the way back, I ate and listened to the surgeon and Nick discuss plans for the shearing. The surgeon did most of the talking. I supposed his confident tone must have been a lot like the one he used in his profession before operating. It seemed to be sufficient for Nick, who mostly nodded and maneuvered the skiff to avoid the chop.

When we got to the lodge, I asked if they needed any help. The surgeon shook his head and said they'd be fine. Nick told me to come around to watch if I wanted. I saw Jim down by the barn leading the last of the alpacas into the corral. I could hear him clicking to it softly.

I went up to my cabin and laid down for what I planned to be a fifteen-minute nap, but didn't open my eyes again until I heard someone shout, "We gotta show this one who's goddamn boss!" I glanced at my watch and saw that I'd been asleep for almost an hour.

I looked out the window toward the corral. The three cream-colored alpacas were already shorn, prancing along the reaches of it. Strange-looking to begin with, they now appeared even odder: completely bald except for their heads and the portion of the ankles above the hoof. A boy Nick used as a deckhand was filling a burlap sack with the last of their fur; a dozen or so sacks like it leaned against the barn wall. Jim was slowly circling the big brown alpaca in the middle of the corral while the surgeon gestured angrily with what looked like a barber's electric clippers. Nick stood off a little ways outside the corral leaning against the fence. I could see him smiling. Dark clouds had rolled in from the north.

I roused myself, went down the hill, and stood next to Nick. He gave me a clap on the shoulder and said, "Well, you missed most of the fun, pal. The job's just about done."

"How's it gone so far?"

"Piece of cake." He nodded toward the corral. 'Our gal here is putting up a bit of a fight. No surprise there."

Jim was walking the big brown alpaca towards the corner of the corral where it met the barn. The surgeon was already waiting there with belts. "Just grab her and hold her against the fence!" he shouted. "We'll have to strap this one in!"

I wasn't sure what I was seeing in Jim's eyes, but it wasn't happy. He shuffled the brown into the corner.

"Jim wants to go easy with her because she's pregnant," Nick said quietly to me. "He treats them like they're his pets. Just like he treats the dogs."

The surgeon stepped up behind the big animal,

wrapped his arms around the middle, and began wrestling her against the fence. The alpaca made a strange bleating noise; the first sound I'd heard from any of them, bared her yellow teeth, and turned her head toward the surgeon.

"Grab her goddamn neck!" the surgeon shouted.

Jim did as he was told, it seemed to me, reluctantly. He tried to keep his face in her line of sight and whispered, "Shh, girl, shh."

The surgeon slipped once on the wet grass, swore, steadied himself, and managed to strap her middle to the fence with one of the belts before cinching it tight. He did the same with her neck. The alpaca kicked at him once hard, and he jumped out of the way.

"Ride 'em, cowboy," Nick called, laughing, but the surgeon wasn't smiling.

I heard Jim say, "Do you need to do that? We didn't with the others."

"This one's pissing me off," the surgeon said. "Not taking any chances. Hold her rump against the fence."

Jim moved to the rear of the alpaca, held her haunches, and turned his head away. The surgeon wasted no time starting the clippers, running them first over the lower part of the alpaca's long neck. As he did, she continued to squirm and thrash. The thick fur fell in clumps onto the grass. There was nothing technical about the clipping itself; the surgeon just moved methodically up and down with studied focus. He moved next to the hind end and worked back towards the front of the animal. When he got to the brown's middle, she began bucking her head so desperately that the fence shook and wood splintered.

The surgeon finished quickly, turned off the clippers and knocked them against the heel of his hand shaking the excess fur loose. "Move up and hold her around the middle until I get these belts loose," he told Jim.

Jim nodded, shifted his grip forward, but kept his head down.

The surgeon set the clippers on a fencepost, loosened the belt around the heavy, low middle of the alpaca, and pulled it free. Her legs wobbled. When he got to the belt on the neck, he said, "Easy now." I wasn't sure if he was talking to the animal or Jim.

He pulled off the last belt and stepped back. "All right," he told Jim. "Let her go."

Jim took his hands away and for a second the big animal swayed, then the legs buckled towards the fence and the rest of her fell over in the opposite direction into her own carpet of fur. She made a short thud when she landed. She lay completely still there in the low light.

I heard Nick say, "Jesus H. Christ."

He straightened next to me. For a moment, no one else moved. Then Jim knelt next to the alpaca and ran his hand gently from the base of the skull down to the top of the back. He turned and looked from the surgeon to Nick and said simply, "Broke her neck."

He looked back down at the brown, his shoulders fell, he shook his head. Nick ducked under the railing of the fence and I followed him up to the animal. The deckhand stood completely still in the barn's opening, the sack dangling from his fingers.

The surgeon had knelt next to the alpaca. We watched his hands make the same trip down the animal's neck, then over her middle. He looked up at Nick and asked, "How far along was she?"

Nick shrugged. "Maybe a few months."

The surgeon nodded slowly, stood up, wiped his hands together. "That's that, then," he said. "We lost 'em both."

I heard a motor faintly approaching on the water, then the sound of distant laughter. I turned and saw one of the lodge's fishing boats coming around the point in the distance.

"Well," Nick said evenly, "it won't do to have her lying here when the guests return. Let's get her in the back of the truck and bury her off in the woods somewhere."

He went around the barn where the vehicles were parked. No one said anything. The deckhand just stood there. The surgeon wound the belts into coils. Jim stayed kneeling, shaking his head back and forth. I turned away and watched the boat make its slow, distant approach towards the dock.

Nick came around the corner of the barn in one of the pick-up trucks. The deckhand opened the wide corral gate, and Nick drove up alongside the alpaca. He jumped out, came back to us, and let down the tailgate. He'd already put a shovel and pickaxe into the back. He said, "I guess we all just take a spot and lift. See how that works."

We did that and began lifting on no particular cue. The animal was heavy, stubby-haired, awkward, but we managed to slide her into the truck's bed. Her eyes were still open, pointing upward. It had begun to drizzle.

"I'll take her," Jim said.

Nick nodded and said, "Fine." He turned to the deckhand and told him, "Get the rest of that fur bagged before the boats come in."

The surgeon said, "If we'd had a proper shearing

pen and equipment, that wouldn't have happened."

I watched Nick regard him. I suppose he was weighing the options of how to reply. After a long moment, he looked at the surgeon and me and said, "The two of you head up to the lodge and get a drink. I'll go meet the boats and join you later."

The surgeon said, "That sounds good to me. I could use a drink."

I said, "I'll give Jim a hand."

Nick looked towards the water and shrugged. I don't think he really cared what we did as long as the mess was cleared away before the rest of the guests came back up the hill from fishing. I watched him climb back through the fence and head down to the dock. Jim was already in the cab behind the wheel. I climbed in the other side and he drove away slowly, the wipers whacking. I didn't look back.

We drove in silence along the same road I'd walked on the day before. I looked over once, but Jim's face was blank. We drove along the bluff until we came to the spot with what had looked like old abandoned farm buildings to me; Jim pulled into a field there and stopped the truck. He got out and immediately started swinging the pickaxe in the earth. He didn't say a word. I waited for him to clear himself some space, then started digging with the shovel behind him. He'd chosen a good place; the dirt was soft and loamy.

After a half-hour, I was sweating and breathing hard. My palms had blistered, but Jim didn't slow down and neither did I. We continued until we had a hole that I assumed Jim thought was big enough because he tossed away the pickaxe and pushed the cap back on his head. He took a bandana from his jeans pocket and blew his nose once loud. He didn't look at me, but I could see he'd been crying.

"Well," he said, "let's get it done."

He backed the truck up against the hole and we slid the alpaca into it. Jim closed her eyes. Then we covered her, Jim using the side of the pickaxe, me the shovel. It only took a few minutes. I realized that it had stopped raining. We tossed the tools in the back of the truck and Jim slammed the tailgate. He stood looking over the clearing.

I said, "That digging could have been worse."

"We used to grow poppies here," he said. "Good spot. Compost pile was right about where the front bumper is."

"You raised around here?"

"He shook his head. "Nebraska. Nebraska and Iowa, but Nebraska mostly."

I thought about that and watched him go around his side of the truck. I did some quick mental math. He climbed back in and started the engine.

We didn't talk on the way back until we were almost to the lodge. Then Jim said, "The son of a bitch never even said he was sorry. He never uttered a word of apology, did he?"

I shook my head. "Not that I remember."

Dinner that night was essentially more of the same: cocktails and appetizers, Nick's positive spin on the day and plan for the next, the wine descriptions, the chef's culinary preview.

There were a couple exceptions. First, the beer folks were a little further gone than before. I granted that to final night festiveness. Off color jokes abounded.

The second was the weather. The clouds had lifted and the evening was like our first: quiet, full of wide, dappled light. A few wispy clouds tinted the color of cranberries as the sun settled among them hung over the charcoal-shaded mountains across the channel. Looking out the window while I ate, the light seemed to fall like a long sigh.

I excused myself during dessert and took a nearly full bottle of red wine off the buffet. I went downstairs with it and out the swinging screen door toward the barn. Cicadas called in the weeds. The tide was creeping in, running along the shore, crackling in the rocks.

I didn't know which of the staff's quarters may have been Jim's, but as it turned out, I didn't need to. I stopped at the entrance to the barn and found him sitting against a post inside scratching one of the smaller alpacas behind the ears. Its head was on his lap. The other two were eating hay from troughs nearby. Jim held a smoldering cigarette in his scratching hand and a plastic travel-mug in the other. I cleared my throat softly and he looked up.

"Shouldn't be smoking in here," I said.

"Point taken."

He sucked on the cigarette a last time and snuffed it out at the creosote-soaked base of the post. I took a couple of steps inside the barn. The light was low. I smelled the twang of manure in the back of my nose.

"Brought this," I said and held the wine bottle out towards him.

Jim shook his head, lifted the travel-mug, and said, "Way ahead of you."

I walked over and sat on a hay bale. I took a swallow from the bottle and said, "They look like something out of a Dr. Seuss book, don't they?"

Jim gave a chuckle and nodded, but didn't

respond. One of the eating alpacas snorted. A few thin sunbeams crept almost horizontal through the barn's slats, dust floating in them.

"So," I said. "I guess you came up here about '70, '71?"

His hand stopped scratching, but he kept his eyes on it. He mumbled, "Thereabouts."

"You come to beat the system or beat the draft?"

Jim looked at me, considering, I suppose. He said, "Both, I guess. Mostly the later. I tried going Conscientious Objector, but no luck. My dad was an ex-Marine, wanted me in the officer-training route." He paused, studying me, his almond-shaped eyes damp at the edges. He said, "You're old enough to know."

I nodded. "I got a low draft number is all. Dumb luck."

He said, "Well, I didn't get so lucky. Tell the truth, I was flat out scared. A friend of mine in the same situation was coming up, so I just went with him. We crossed together; he went to Toronto, I came west. Heard about this place, the farm, from a girl in Edmonton. Been here, really, ever since."

I took a turn at nodding. I looked up at the rafters in the shadows, curved like the bottom of a canoe.

"I hung those," Jim said looking where I was. "Stoned most of the time, if I remember correctly."

We both laughed. We were quiet for a while. Jim went back to scratching, sipping from his mug. The music at the lodge changed to swing. I could hear chairs sliding out of the way. I listened to that, to the water in the rocks, to the alpacas breathing.

Finally, Jim said, "Talk about dumb luck. Day before I left, I was protesting about the bombing raids in Cambodia with a big group of people in downtown

Minneapolis. Buddy I was with got a crooked hair and set off a stick of dynamite against a corner of the post office." He shook his head. "I had no idea what he was doing. I was in some bushes next to him taking a leak. But he grabbed me afterwards and we ran." Jim stopped scratching, put his head back, took a sip from his mug. He said, "I read about myself in the newspaper the next morning before we crossed over up near the Boundary Waters. Fair amount of damage, no one hurt. Federal offense, though."

I sat looking at him. I asked, "So, the Ford amnesty? The Carter pardon?"

He shook his head. "Moot point with my warrant outstanding."

I frowned and said, "You got to be kidding."

He held up his mug as if to toast, took a sip, said, "Wish I was."

Someone had turned the music up in the lodge. I heard happy shouting and the pounding of dancing feet. It was warm in the barn. I took a couple more swallows of wine, then just sat there.

A minute or two passed before I asked, "You in touch with anyone from home?"

He said quietly, "A sister."

"You ever think of trying to go back anyway?"

He shrugged. "Hell, I'm fifty-nine. Too old to chance prison. My brother's a Vietnam War vet, an angry one. Dad was career military; he's never forgiven me either. Only he's in a home now with Alzheimer's." He spit into the dirt. "My mom's on her last legs. Hooked up to a bunch of tubes in a hospital."

I looked at him sitting there. I wondered if we might have become friends when we were younger. I wasn't sure. I took another swallow from the bottle; he did the same from his mug.

He looked up at me. "And then there's the fact that I think I'm a father. To be honest, I'm almost sure of it. My sister let me know that the girl I'd been seeing at the time had a baby not long after I left. A boy."

The light in the barn had fallen; it was musty, quiet. After a while, I could hear Jim drink, but could barely see him. A few frogs began to groan outside. I drank, too. At some point afterwards, I said goodnight, found my way up to my cabin, got in bed, and thought some more. It was that last thing he said that really got to me. I didn't fall asleep for a long time.

I skipped the wake-up call. I rolled over, tried to go back to sleep, but couldn't. I waited until I heard the boats depart, then dressed and headed to the lodge. I ate a muffin and drank coffee on the deck while I waited for the horizon to brighten and the lights to come on up at Nick's house. When they did, I waited a decent amount of time, then walked up there and knocked on the door. He met me in his bathrobe, one of the same green-plaid kind that hung in each cabin, and asked me in. He was toweling his hair, fresh from the shower. He didn't look so young that way.

We sat down and I told him my idea. He listened, holding the towel still in his hands. Once I'd finished, he looked over my shoulder towards the water, then back at me and said, "Go ahead. Do what you want. If you get into trouble, don't turn to me. I need someone here to look after the place when I head south tomorrow, and it doesn't much matter whether it's him or you." To be honest, I'd expected some sort of rancor or, at least, surprise from him. But Nick was customarily matter of fact.

I went down to the barn. Jim wasn't inside and

wasn't around the staff housing. I found him over by the garden, hosing out some plastic buckets. He had the cup end of a thermos steaming with coffee on the grass next to him. He turned off the hose, but left the coffee alone.

I told him the same version I'd given to Nick, except I added that he was free to use my condo and car, stay as long as necessary; my new neighbors didn't know me anyway. My bank paid all my bills electronically. I kept a debit/credit card and gave Jim the others, my driver's license, passport, plane ticket, and the keys to my car and condo. He opened the passport and glanced at the photo. When he closed it and our eyes met, I knew he thought we looked enough alike, too; that it would work.

I said, "In Nanaimo on the way up, they only radioed customs. No one even came down to the dock. I bet they're just as slack going back. Might stick a head in the plane, ask the purpose of the trip, stuff like that. You just take the last plane, sit in the back, shove a lodge hat over your head, act like any other asshole from Chicago. Guests ask, tell them you're going down for some end-of-the-season errands. They inquire about me, say I'm staying to spend some time with my old friend, Nick. They won't ask; won't happen."

He looked down at the items in his hand for a while as if weighing them. Finally, he said, "If I went, I'd just go long enough to say goodbye...you know, try to look up my son, take care of some things."

I said, "There's no rush."

He said, "I can't guarantee there won't be problems."

I nodded and said, "I think you should try."

He looked out over the water, where or at what,

I could only guess. Then he asked, "Nick okay with this?"

I nodded again.

"God almighty," he muttered and shook his head. "This is a hell of a thing you're doing."

"We all get dealt cards," I told him. "Let's exchange money."

He gave me the Canadian cash he had. It wasn't much, but I was sure I wouldn't need a lot more. Nick had accounts at the stores in the village he'd said I could use, as well as several more over on Vancouver Island. I had that card of my own I'd kept. What else did I need?

In the end, I sent him to shave his stubble, clean up, and get packed just as the boats were coming back in. They had finished their little run to pull crab and shrimp pots before the floatplanes arrived. That way everyone would go home with catch, even those who hadn't landed a fish; everyone would head back happy.

I didn't go down to the dock for the farewell. I watched from my cabin window as they took group photos and listened to their bursts of laughter. I heard Nick say something about the last trip of the season, what a great group they were, that he'd see them again next year. Then he had the staff pass out handsome tweed satchels as gifts, each with the lodge's name and a jumping fish stenciled on the side. I stayed long enough to see the planes leave, Jim on the last one.

The rest of the staff took their leave over the course of the afternoon. The college girls all went on the late afternoon ferry over to Port McNeil for the drive south on Vancouver Island. I guess a few of them saw me around, but no one said anything. I suppose Nick gave them the same explanation I'd suggested to

Jim. Anyway, they were anxious to get on to the next chapter in their lives, that was plain to see.

Nick had me up to his place that evening. We bar-b-qued hamburgers, ate on his wrap-around deck, and drank beer while the sun made its slow descent. He told me some more about the problems with his own marriage, his ideas about possibly making Tucson a more permanent home. After dinner, he took me on a tour of his place, explained the circuit breakers, procedures with the animals, where the keys were kept, and the like. I slept in his guest room, which would quickly become my home for an uncertain amount of time.

Early the next morning before his floatplane came, I walked the grounds with Nick. We brought the boats up into a storage area behind the barn except for the skiff, in case I wanted to use it myself. I walked down to the dock with him before he left. He gave me a quick hug and called me stupid this and stupid that. We made vague plans for me to drive over to his place in Tucson from Santa Fe to visit. Then he boarded and we waved as they motored away from the dock. I looked after the plane until it had lifted and disappeared from sight. It was another clear, clean day, warm, hardly a cloud in the sky. My heart had steadied a bit, but I still felt as if I was in a dream. It wasn't unpleasant.

That was almost three months ago now. As I say, sitting here, snow falling, circumstances seem unlikely but somehow symmetric. I haven't heard from Jim, that's true. I don't actually know how to get in touch with him. We didn't exchange numbers, and I never even had the chance to install a phone in my new place, but it's unlikely he's there anyway. I suppose I could contact Nick, but I doubt he knows either. At any rate, I haven't been inclined to try, nor do I suppose I will.

The fall was wonderful, more colors and drier than might be expected this far north. I took the skiff out a number of times in early October and hit a good run of silvers, all legal. I'm still eating off the fillets I froze. I've recently tried my hand at fishing in some of the streams and have gotten a couple nice early steelheads.

As for spending time, I located the high-quality art materials Nick told me his wife never used in a closet, and have put those to good use. I paint daily for several hours, which I haven't done since college; it's wonderful, like discovering an old friend. The lodge has a whole library of books of which I've only cracked the surface. I found a couple of manuals there on local fauna. I've hiked a good portion of the island identifying things. I have some seedlings started in the greenhouse next to the garden; that's a first for me. I go into the village on one of the bikes or in the truck when I need to, and have taken the ferry over to Port McNeil a few times. I guess what I enjoy as much as anything is just sitting on Nick's deck studying the tides and watching the landscape change, watching the winter approach. Then there are the dogs and alpacas for company, who I've grown to love.

Mostly, the primary difference I see between what I might be doing in Santa Fe and here is one of purpose; in Santa Fe, I'd only be searching for one. We've recently had this little powdering of snow that has softened things, quieted them, added stillness. And with the colder weather, the Aurora Borealis is like a symphony. This is a beautiful place. I'm fine.

If you were to ask me, I'd still say I'm certain Jim is coming back. Perhaps his parents' illnesses have become prolonged. Or maybe he's established some sort of relationship with his son. I hope he has. Like I say, life takes its twists and turns. Forty years is a long time. There's really no hurry. I'd probably be fine if Jim didn't return until next fishing season. In a pinch, I could learn to guide. Heck, if pressed, I could probably stay indefinitely without much trouble at all.

Kevin Stadt

Keep away from People

"Daddy needs some alone time." That's what I said to my ten-year-old son, Nick, that warm spring Saturday when the world fell apart.

"Come on, Dad. Let's go see a movie. I don't feel like staying home. And anyway, I'm too old for a babysitter." Nick tried to give me the puppy dog eyes. My heart ached at how much he looked like a perfect mix of me and his mom, with her dark complexion and my freckles and gangly frame. Guilt knotted in my gut, the guilt of spending time doing something for myself. The guilt of being the parent that lived.

But I left him so I could spend the afternoon working on my stupid novel. I'd only been at a Starbucks in Naperville for an hour, and was brainstorming ways to make my protagonist more likable when the screaming started. I squinted out the front window to see—*something*—pulling a man up into a tree across the street and a woman on the sidewalk shrieking, her purse and shopping bag on the ground.

I raced to the glass door, my heart pumping waves of warm adrenaline. A six-foot-long millipede with hundreds of spidery, thin legs yanked the man into a tree. Two huge, black pincers in the front balanced out an arched stinger at the other end.

It backed up an elm tree holding the guy by the ankles with its pincers. He reached out toward the woman and shouted, "Karen!" and the thing snapped its stinger into his neck. He tensed up for a second, and then his arms dropped slack.

But he wasn't dead or even unconscious. I guess the sting paralyzed him from the neck down. His eyes got even wider and his shouts became more frantic. One of the other customers had opened the door, so I heard him clearly even over the blood thudding in my ears.

"Holy Christ, Karen, oh my God what the fuck someone help me Jesus don't just stand there–"

The creature dragged him to a high branch. Then, with the guy squealing nonstop, it crawled circles around him while working webbing out of its back end with a pair of extra-long legs near its tail, wrapping him tightly.

People yelled, took pictures and video, called 911, ran to their cars. Karen passed out.

Once he'd been wrapped, the thing started eating. Settled right on top of him and chewed on his face. Its mandibles ripped into his cheek, his neck, and then worked with extra excitement when it got to his eyes. The guy alive, awake, screaming the whole time.

I sprinted to my car and almost crashed a dozen times on the way home. It was the same story everywhere, the radio said. I called home over and over, but no answer. When I got there, the sitter was gone and Nick shook in a fetal position under the bed.

After that, we found out just how fragile society really was.

The governments tried to hold it together at

first, but the news reported that deaths by bugs ran into millions globally every day. They came straight out of the ground anywhere with no warning. Their hard exoskeletons made them tough to kill unless you got a clean headshot—no easy task, given how fast and erratically they moved. Worse still, the sheer numbers of creatures swarming the heavily populated areas utterly overwhelmed the police and military. Away from the cities, people hid, hoarded, and fought. Suddenly one morning, you couldn't get gas anymore. Static replaced the news and the power went off. You went to the store for supplies and found your neighbors shooting each other over Spam.

For a while we tried to hunker down at home. One day we went out in the back yard to pee. We stood back to back near the old oak, talking about what we'd cook over a fire for dinner, when Nick screamed. I hadn't heard anything coming, no warning. By the time I turned around, warm piss going down my leg, a hole in the ground had appeared where Nick had been and the creature had already pulled him halfway up the tree. I drew the revolver I'd taken to wearing at all times, but I knew with the thing zigzagging, I might hit my son. So I steadied myself and tracked them in my sights as the bug went to a high branch and began webbing. After it immobilized him, the creature neared his face and took just a slight pause, as if debating which part to eat first.

I put one of its black eyes in my sights, let out a breath, and squeezed the cold metal trigger. The crack echoed in my ears, the smell of gunpowder filled the air, and the creature dropped to the ground.

That was the only one I've ever succeeded in killing. It took me an hour to get Nick out of the webbing and back down the tree. He didn't talk for two days.

We took off, leaving our home in the suburbs behind to find a safer place, bullshitting ourselves that there was such a thing. At least staying on the move felt like we were doing something, taking action. Talked to a lot of people on the road. Heard plenty of crazy stories and theories. Some say they're aliens. Or ancient animals that were under us all along, dormant in the Earth.

Some say they're from hell, sent to punish us.

I don't know. But I did notice pretty early that every time people grouped up at a supposedly secure military safe zone or whatever, they got swarmed. Then one day Nick and I walked past a high school in West Chicago and saw huge words scrawled in red spray paint on the brick wall.

They never take people who are alone.

We stared at the message, frozen at the thought. Nick squeezed my hand. "That's not true, is it?"

"I don't know. No. Just some crazy guy with paint."

"We won't split up, right?" He looked even more terrified than the day it all began.

I hugged him. "Are you kidding? I need to stick with you so you can protect me. No way I'm ditching my bodyguard."

Nick buried his face in my sweater, his shoulders jerking with the muffled sobs. I tried to reassure him. "Don't worry, buddy. I won't leave you, ever. No matter what."

But that night, as we camped out on the floor of a Walgreens, in the candy and snack aisle, I couldn't sleep. I listened to Nick's breathing, my ears straining to catch the sounds of digging or scratching beneath us. Could those things really be passing over single individuals? I thought back to all the times I'd seen people taken. Had any of them ever been alone, or were they always snatched from a pair or group?

My stomach turned sour with nausea and dizziness washed over me. I realized they were always with other people, the ones who'd been taken. Every time. Which explained why the governments' responses—groups of soldiers, groups of police, groups of health care workers—had been such catastrophes. Over the next few weeks, the message spread, scrawled on billboards, houses, pavement.

Don't congregate in groups.

Stay away from people!

They won't take you if you're alone.

We had to face reality. At first, I tried to make a deal with Nick, that we'd stay apart but within eyeshot. He'd be alone, but not far away. I could still make food or a campfire and leave it for him, write notes or yell to him.

But he was just a terrified kid. After a few days of separation, I'd always wake up in the morning to find he'd come during the night and curled up next to me.

Then one night, I woke up in the upstairs master bedroom of some random McMansion in Wheaton, my ears pricking up at the sound of a lamp getting knocked over downstairs. My hand grabbed the revolver and my feet took me to the bedroom door. I lay flat and peeked through the railing to see three of them skittering among the living room furniture downstairs, testing the air with their antennae.

We went out the window, the creatures right behind us, and ran until fire burned in our chests. This happened again and again.

That's when I knew. I had to leave him alone. I

had to. Right? Is that right?

One night after he fell asleep, I put all our food in the backpack, along with the gun and shells, and left everything next to him. I knelt over him, my hand trembling, a sickness opening in my gut so horrible I have no word to name it, the periphery of my vision blurring and pulsing with my hammering heartbeat.

I wrote a note, drawing the pen heavily across the paper, each letter a quiet nightmare, knowing full well what losing his mother in a car accident three years before had done to him, knowing that this would be in many ways worse.

Nick,

You have to be strong, buddy. Be careful and keep away from people. Please. Just stay alive. That's all that matters. When this is over, I'll wait for you back at our house, okay? We'll see each other again.

Please understand. The only thing I want more than to be with you is to protect you.

I have to do this. You're the whole world to me.

I love you so much. So much.

Dad

I don't know how long I stood there watching him sleep before I left. A pretty long time. It was only then that I fully realized what they'd taken from us. Maybe they really were from hell, or maybe hell had come to Earth. How else can I explain a monster that hunts us in precisely the way that hurts us most, other than as some kind of divine punishment? Don't most predators favor the lone prey over the herd?

I tried to keep an eye on him from a safe

distance, hidden. He woke up in the morning, frantically searched and called for me. I lay in the dirt behind some bushes, clutching the cold binoculars, holding myself to the spot with gritted teeth, hot tears streaming down my face. Nick read the note and tore it up. He fell to his knees, sobbing and punching the ground.

He didn't eat for three days. I started to go to him a dozen times, but I said to myself, do you want to kill your son?

Then one day I couldn't find him. I'd made a fireless camp hidden about three-quarters of a mile away, as usual, watching him with binoculars. He made his own camp under the bridge by a small creek. I watched until he went to sleep, and long after. But when I woke up, he was just gone.

"No, no, no..." I ran to the spot, my breaths coming short and shallow. I screamed his name, spent the rest of the day tracking the creek in both directions, then going in big concentric circles to sweep the area, until I collapsed. No trace. I told myself I'd find him the next day, but I think even then I knew it was a purely functional fiction, a bulwark against losing my mind.

That was almost three years ago. He would be thirteen now. Is thirteen.

Three years of searching. Leaving messages on walls, trees, and signs: *Nick, are you okay? I need to know. I love you. I'm so sorry. Please don't hate me.*

There has never been word back, but I keep going because maybe there will be a day when the monsters are gone and I see Nick again back at the house. I pray that day comes. And that he understands why I did it. Maybe even forgives me.

I've had enough alone time.

Larry Handy

Mrs. Meriwether

"He who loses his dreaming is lost."
—Australian Aborigine

act i. greetings

Jeff Baucus didn't want the burden of his mother-in-law moving in so he sent her to a retirement home where the old go to die. His wife Sidney had been depressed since her father died. Her mother Lilly was bound to a wheelchair. Though she hated the idea at first of sending her mother away she realized that taking care of 3 daughters and an elderly parent was too much work. A burden.

At Bradley-Bell Retirement home you went to die. There were 75 seniors living there. Lilly's first day was frightening. "We'll come to see you every week, mom." And that particular promise was kept for about a week. Soon the visits went from every week to every other week and then to only once a month.

The Jr. High School children from the local Christian school came to Bradley-Bell every Thursday to sing to the old folks and play bingo with them and ballroom dance with them. And every Thursday Lilly watched from her wheelchair. She couldn't have any pets except fish and birds but she didn't want fish and birds.

Her next room neighbor Helena Bradbury had a grandson named Simon who would come by on his skateboard every afternoon faithfully to visit. Simon began running grocery errands for Lilly as well. She paid him $25. Sometimes she just needed someone young to talk to. Young people have a power of keeping old people alive. Simon was able to do this for quite awhile until his grandmother finally died of a stroke. Soon after, he stopped coming by Bradley-Bell to run errands for Lilly. And she was alone again. Every friend she made at Bradley-Bell she outlived. One died every 5 months. Retirement homes had that effect. When you are around sickness and death you get sick and you die.

Studying the calendar became a strange hobby for Lilly. She stared at it, marking off days. She read the calendar as if it were a novel or a magazine, looking at the future represented by squares and numbers. Christmas, Thanksgiving, Easter, New Years, these were times she would spend with her family, time away from Bradley-Bell. Her birthday she would spend at the retirement home, her family coming to visit her. Elderly and widowed and in a wheelchair this would be the rest of her life.

In her young life she played tennis and was a ballerina. She kicked high and with grace. By the time she turned 50 her arthritis worsened and through the years the cartilage in her knees wore down until it eventually became a bone on bone issue.

Bradley-Bell was a prison where everyone smiled. You met everyone on your first day. The workers gave you a welcome tour. It was a way to help you feel comfortable with your surroundings. One by one they took you to meet each inmate until by the end of the week all faces had seen your face—those without dementia actually remembering your face.

Helen Nakamura was the newbie. She was the only "Oriental" of Bradley-Bell. "Orientals" have a very un-American way of not sending their elderly parents to retirement homes. Their parents actually lived with them and their children, multigenerational homes being a reality. But, by outliving her husband and son it created an "un-Oriental" situation for her forcing her into the status of inmate. Helen Nakamura moved into Helena Bradbury's old room that had been vacant for a long time. Farewell Helena hello Helen and Lilly now had a new next room neighbor.

In the recreation room there was pool and ping pong and even pinball. For those not committed to "recreate" there was the garden area where there were chairs and chess and chitchatting. Music was a common pleasure at Bradley-Bell. None of that loud crazy young person's music. Just Bach and Charlie Parker and Stravinsky and Miles—cool Miles, not fusion Miles—and occasionally the Beach Boys.

Lilly wheeled her chair around the rec-room, Miles Davis' song "So What" was in the air. She couldn't dance but she could spin in circles, still full of life. She didn't like the idea of electric scooters, she loved using her shoulders and hands. For those that could remember her name it was the familiar greetings of: "Hey there, Lilly", "Afternoon Ms. Meriwether". The hip oldsters even shouted out, "What's happening."

Rolling out of the recreation room and into the garden area was like turning a page. A well landscaped lawn with a Victorian fountain, it was a pleasant place to keep one's sanity or loose it. Olga Peara, the former soloist whose music was featured in dozens of obscure Italian films, sat under the oak in the west end of the garden playing her viola. Her audience always consisted of the same three ladies. Rolling past Olga, Lilly came to a table where she watched an entire checker match being played with chess pieces. Next to that odd arrangement, sat Helen Nakamura the newcomer folding pieces of paper rather rapidly.

She had a unique gift of looking off into the distance, her eyes wandering in all directions except where her hands were. She turned simple sheets of paper into intricate birds, all sizes of cranes.

"You make one thousand of these and your wish will come true," she said to Lilly who she never looked at. She seemed to just sense that she was around, or maybe she just heard the squeaking of the wheelchair wheels.

"Is that Oriental?" Lilly asked.

"It's Japanese. It's origami. Oriental is for rugs," Helen responded shutting her eyes. Her fingers moved rapidly.

"What city in Japan were you born in?" Lilly asked.

"Cincinnati. Ohio. United States of America," Helen answered. "What city in Japan were you born in?" she returned the question to Lilly.

"Oh."

"Yeah. Oh." Helen finished folding a crane and added it to the pile of birds on her left.

"Are you trying to make a wish?" Lilly asked.

"Sure am. I wish I could get the hell out of here."

"You must keep your grandchildren entertained with your paper folding."

"I don't have any grandkids."

"Oh."

"Yeah. Oh."

"Do you do Taikey as well? That's something I'd like to learn. I wonder if they have it for people in wheelchairs."

"You mean the Taiko drums? No, I don't play those. I suppose people in wheelchairs could play them. I don't know. They're very large. You have to hit them with both arms and at the same time not be able to roll away in your chair."

"I didn't know there were any drums used. I thought you just moved your arms around like you were swimming in the air. I see Oriental Japanese do it all the time on television when they are in the park. They all move in unison sort of like ballet. It's so beautiful."

Helen finished another crane. She opened her eyes, stared at Lilly and shook her head. "Taikey? You mean Tai Chi?"

"Is that what it's called?"

Helen never answered back.

"Why do you close your eyes when you fold the paper?" Lilly asked.

"Because I'm wishing. I close my eyes when I make a wish. And Tai Chi is Chinese not Japanese. And Oriental is for rugs."

"Oh."

"Yeah. Oh."

"Do you think you can teach me how to make those?"

"No."

"Oh."

"Yeah. Oh."

Lilly left Helen to fold her cranes at the table. The rest of the day carried on as it was meant to carry on.

Back in her room she went through old photographs of her ballet days, her tennis days. Darn that wheel chair. Darn those knees. Memories of better days made her sick, and that evening, she didn't eat when the rest of the inmates of Bradley-Bell ate.

The next morning she saw Helen at the same table in the garden folding more cranes.

"What can I pay you to teach me how to do that?" Lilly asked. "The errand boy who used to skateboard around here I paid him $25 dollars."

"You should find him and pay him to teach you," Helen replied.

"He wasn't Oriental."

"Neither am I. Oriental is a rug. I'm American."

"Oh."

"Yeah. Oh."

"Can I at least watch you?"

"Yes, but from far away."

"Oh."

"Yeah. Oh."

Helen's fingers were quick and mechanical. She folded paper as if she were crocheting. Lilly motioned her fingers in the air while watching her, trying to pick up the folds. Though Helen's eyes were closed the entire time, deep in her wish-trance, she could tell what was going on. The next day and the next day after were the same.

"Keep saying Oriental without talking about a rug and you will never learn how to fold wishing cranes from me."

"Oh."

"Yeah. Oh."

"What shall I call you then?"

"Friend. And then act like it."

"Oh."

"Yeah. Oh."

"I brought some paper of my own. I've been practicing a little in my room. I kind of have it." Lilly showed Helen a few folds. "It's tricky."

Helen shook her head. "This isn't about paper planes. This is about paper birds. Here, let me show you the right way. You can fold one bird in twenty five folds." Helen took out a new piece of paper and began folding. "Watch me, I'll fold slow so you can see. Watch! And then I'll give you a paper and then we will fold slowly and together."

After folding 6 cranes together, Lilly got more proficient.

"You need special paper to fold cranes, you know," Helen said. "But you can use any paper except the kind you wipe your butt with."

Another day in the garden ended, and Lilly rolled back into her room. She began folding paper cranes while listening to her favorite music, while looking at old photographs, while sitting in silence. She kept folding until her fingers began to stiffen. She feared for her hands as she had once feared for her knees, the knees that got her in the wheel chair. "I wish I could walk without hurting. I wish I could run. I wish I could dance. I wish I didn't need this damn chair!" Though her fingers stiffened she kept folding until she fell asleep at her desk.

act ii. beatings

It took a rainy day to keep them out of the garden. Only the truly insane stood in the rain...with the watchful eye of the orderlies, of course. There were people like Mr. Murray who would stand in the center of the garden lawn holding a black umbrella. He loved puddles. He loved ripples. He lost his wife and his right leg. People like the Evans twins. Elsa and Eunice both 67, both in the same retirement home, both were married to the same man but at different times. A total rarity. They both loved the scent of a wet day. Everyone else at Bradley-Bell crowded into the recreation room when it rained. A few sat on the front porch but never too long. Folks liked to admire the sound of rain from inside their shelter

Helen and Lilly hadn't become real close until it rained.

"I have a large table in my room we can fold our cranes there." Lilly said.

Helen kept her origami papers in a briefcase. She stepped foot inside Lilly's room for the first time and shook her head.

"You don't take your shoes off inside?"

"Why? Do you want me to?"

"I just thought that Orientals—oh. Never mind."

Helen gave Lilly a mean look.

"Sorry." Lilly said.

"Go on, say it."

"Oh."

"Yeah. Oh."

"I love the sound of rain."

"It can be both distracting and fulfilling at the same time. When you fold cranes on a rainy day, you think more about the rain than you think about your wish. But then anything from nature is good. Rain is good."

"Your mind never wanders when you fold?"

"Never! I only fold and think about my wish. That's why I can fold with my eyes shut."

"How many cranes have you folded so far?"

"644!"

"That seems so much like a lot."

"It is."

"And you've folded each crane with your eyes closed?"

"Yes!"

"Why are you always yelling when you speak?"

"Why are you always asking questions when you speak?"

"Oh."

"Yeah. Oh."

Outside the window the rain would beat and then it would pound and then it would tap and then it would brush and then it would shower and then it would splash and then it would sort of sing and the wind would howl and add to it. The skies really wept.

"Set yourself a goal," Helen said to Lilly. "Do 1000 cranes in one season. Winter is coming. There are 3 months December, January, February. 11 cranes a day by the end of winter, you'll have a 1000. Spring is good for new beginnings. Things bloom in the spring. If you wish hard enough your wish will bloom in the spring. But you must put your mind to it."

"Do you have to make 1000 cranes by yourself?" Lilly asked. "Can't you have someone to help you to fold? Someone helping you to help make your wish come true?"

"No! You have to do it all by yourself. It's like a quest. A personal journey. When your fingers hurt from folding, when you cut them on the edge of the paper, wish harder! Pain puts power into the wish."

"What about laughter?"

"No laughter—just shut up and keep folding!"

"Oh."

Lilly could not shut her eyes to fold. It was

too much of an unreal thing to do. Her mind would wander off into other things. The sound of the rain. How it reminded her of her childhood in Missouri where she'd sit on her father's lap while they both sat on the porch. Rain would bead on a leaf then after enough beads the leaf would bend and the droplets rolled off. As a young girl she feared the rain until her father sat and watched it with her. He wanted her to love the rain, love the fear away. These were years and decades—it seemed like a century ago—but felt like only a week. The picture on her wall of her dancing in contrast to the wheel chair she was in strengthened her focus and she folded with more intensity.

Helen was methodical. She seemed to keep in rhythm with the rain and the lightning that followed. After folding 4 cranes, lightning would strike at the exact moment she finished every succeeding crane. 25 folds. Done. Lightning. 25 folds. Done. Lightning. And then again and then again.

"I like your room," Helen said breaking the silence. "It's not as clean as the garden outside but I like it." She finished a crane and thunder rolled. She took another piece of paper and began folding. Rain beat even harder. She shut her eyes and breathed.

"Thank you." Lilly said.

Helen finished another crane and lightning struck again.

"I'm going to finish 1000 by the beginning of spring," Lilly said.

"Do it!"

Two days before Thanksgiving, Lilly got a call from her daughter asking her to join the family for the holidays. She hadn't heard from her daughter in months. Granted, it would only be for the weekend and she would have to sleep in the living room on the fold away bed, but it was better than spending the holidays alone. She took her daughter up on the offer.

Four minutes after the conversation with her daughter, Lilly heard a knock at the door. It was Helen.

"Do you want to go to a restaurant for Thanksgiving? I like Soul food. It's the closest American food to Oriental food. But don't call me Oriental—that word is for rugs. And it's called Soul food not Negro food."

"My daughter just called and invited me to spend Thanksgiving with the family. I'm going to see my grandkids."

"Oh." Helen said in a low voice. Her eyes moved to the direction of the floor.

"I'm sorry. We can go have dinner when I get back from my daughter's."

"I'm going to fold some more cranes in my room." She left.

But she didn't fold anything. Helen sat in her room and stared out the window as did many of the other residents of Bradley-Bell.

Thanksgiving came.

"Let me help with the cooking."

"No mom, I've got it. Besides, Jeff will help."

"Oh what does he know about cooking?"

Thanksgiving came and Lilly sat in the corner of the living room while everyone helped prepare the meal. She wasn't allowed even to open the can of cranberry sauce. The Thanksgiving Day parade was on television. Parades never change. No matter how much films have changed or music or even what people eat—who would have ever thought Americans would be eating raw fish?—parades never changed.

Music, costumes and floats one after the other. Then a bad smell filled the house. It was something burning. Her son-in-law Jeff had burned the pumpkin pie. "Oh God! Sorry! Sorry!" Lilly didn't mind for the pie. She preferred apple to pumpkin anyway. The only awful thing was that the pie was on fire and not the son-in-law. There was nothing to do except watch television and wait for dinner. For some reason she felt more free at the retirement home than with her family. She shut her eyes like a Buddhist. But did what old people do when there is nothing to do. Take a nap.

"Wake up, grandma! Wake up! It's time to eat."

At the dinner table she sat in silence staring at her family. As ridiculous at it sound the paper cranes were more of a family to her. They listened. Though they were paper, though they had no brains, no voice, no pulse they listened and treated her with the respect. They didn't through her away. She told them her dreams in each folded crease.

Lilly grew annoyed with the table. There was nothing to give thanks for. In a few days her family would send her back to Bradley-Bell. Everything about her son-in-law's face annoyed her. His eyes. He had a wild man's eyes. Blue eyes like hers but icy eyes. He had a maniac's eyes. His red face annoyed her. The color of a guilty peach. A sissy's blush. And his balding hair that he kept trying to hide by getting a stupid looking crew cut. Didn't work. He was the cause of her being shipped off to that retirement home. She grew annoyed with her daughter for also letting her go. She didn't raise her to be so weak, so vulnerable, so insensitive, she must have learned that in college or back backing through Europe or something. Never under her roof. Never under the roof she and her husband sacrificed for.

"Mom how's everything? The food taste alright?"

"Fine honey. Thank you."

No it wasn't. It was never fine.

Her three granddaughters, so beautiful and a joy to be around reminded her of how old she was. How strange the world was becoming. The three of them moved too quickly, they spoke too quickly; they used new slang words she wasn't up to date with. They played with strange technologies. The world wasn't slow anymore and her granddaughters were the living prancing sign.

Her friend Helen was blunt, and raised her voice when she spoke but after being called *Oriental* times over who wouldn't yell? At least Helen cared about her.

Being alone is not sad. All of those folks at the retirement home who have no family to go home to, no loved ones to spend the holidays with are in luck. Being alone is good. Especially if they have a coward for a daughter and an idiot for a son-in-law. Who wants to eat with a coward and an idiot anyhow? Right? It's better to be alone. It's better to stare at the wall than to stare at how they chew large portions of turkey and pie—grazing at the dinner table. Turkeys eating turkey.

When dinner was over she told her daughter she wanted to go back to Bradley-Bell. When her daughter asked why she simply said "I miss my cranes."

Instead of shopping during black Friday, they took grandma back home.

"So how was your Thanksgiving?" Helen asked. They joined each other in the garden again.

"I brought you some leftovers if you want. Lots of Turkey slices, dressing, potato salad, no pie."

"I'm not big on potato salad or dressing. I'll take the turkey though."

"Well, I got plenty of it. Consolation prize. How was your Oriental Negro food?"

"Soul food. I didn't have any. I didn't want to go by myself. I just ate with the others here. The kids from the school all served us lunch for Thanksgiving. I took extra portions that I shouldn't have and saved it for dinner."

"Did you fold any cranes?"

"No."

"Me neither. I used to love holidays."

"I love the smell of Christmas. Did you hear they're putting up a new tree in a couple of days?"

"How come you're not yelling at me anymore? You normally yell when you speak."

"Well, can't you see? I'm getting old. I'm too tired."

"You're getting old? You're already old." Lilly began folding her first crane of the day. Helen took out a piece of origami paper from her case, she shut her eyes and started wishing away with each fold. "No matter what," Lilly continued, "the next two holidays I'm staying here. Both Christmas and New Years. No matter how much they beg me to visit them."

act iii. fleetings

The first day of the last month of the year came and Bradley-Bell smelled different. Cinnamon and ginger and allspice. It was time for yuletide. Another Christmas season, another end of the year. Another 12 months. Another giant tree in the lobby another angel on top. Another batch of college students from Christian schools who need ministry/charity credit for a class so they are sent to visit lonely old people. Another batch of child carolers. Santa Claus even takes a break from the local mall to spend time with the old-timers. Another holiday fruitcake—yes, people still eat that, even old-timers with no teeth. They don't bite the hard part they "gum" the hard part. Another holiday soundtrack on repeat. Same songs, different versions of the same songs, different voices singing same songs in different versions. Another batch of non-alcoholic eggnog, and another chance to smuggle the good stuff in your room.

"These places are like pounds. Pounds for people. Dogs get put to sleep, people get put to rest. That's why they call these places rest homes."

"Let's fold cranes."

Twenty days later Lilly got the holiday phone call from her daughter. The mom-I-wish-you-a-Merry-Christmas phone call. The mom we'd love to have you over for Christmas phone call. "No, honey," was Lilly's reply. "The girls and I are going to throw an old ladies ball at the retirement center," was lilly's lie-reply. "We're going to have a group of young topless muscle men jump out of a Christmas cake and shake their hips for us, too. We're all so excited about it" – another Lilly lie-reply. "No honey, I'm serious." / "Yes, I know." / "No, honey I am fine. Thank you for the offer but I am happy being here this holiday." / "Yes, I am sure." / "No, I am not upset about Thanksgiving." / "No, I love your husband, Jeff. Jeff is an angel. You married a great man." / "Tell him that bald spot on the top of his head makes him look distinguished. Like a senator." / "He needs to quit that human resources job at the Christian University and run for politics." / "Yes." / "I'll be okay." / "No, you don't have to send me any Christmas gifts" / "I'm thinking about changing my religion anyway." / "I'm becoming Jewish." / "Yes. Jewish. Don't they celebrate Kwanzaa?" / "The day after Christmas?" / "Yes, if you're gonna send me something; send it to me on the 26th." / "I'll be sure to get it then." / "If I'm not hung over from partying with all of those bare-chested fellows—the cake dancers." / "I know." / "What do I want for Kwanzaa? Organ paper." / "Organ paper. For folding paper cranes." / "Organ-what? Organ-gami? Whorey-gamey—honey, I'm too old. My tongue can't pronounce these Oriental words." / "Yeah, I love you too, Sydney." / "Good bye." / "Tell the kids grandma loves them." / "Yes." / "Kisses back." / "Bye." **BITCH.**

Tomato glazed meat loaf for Christmas. Holiday ham—honey glazed holiday ham. No filet mignon. Apple cider, egg nog, hot chocolate, yes. No champagne. No half naked men jumping from a cake just some old-timers moving slow to Benny Goodman. Lots of slices of half eaten apple pie...and dozens upon dozens of paper cranes. Dozens upon dozens of red and pink paper cranes, some green ones too. Helen and Lilly's Cranes. Yuletide made you fold faster. Loneliness makes you fold faster. It makes your fingers reach for something harmful—a bottle or a needle or a pill or it can make you reach for a simple piece of paper. Loneliness can make you do things to that piece of paper. Change it. Make it fly. Give it a head and a tail and wings. Wish after wish. Merry Christmas.

"We should start our own business."

"Why?"

"We should sell these cranes."

"No! No selling!"

"It's just a thought. Maybe little children would like these."

"No!"

"Gee, Helen. I thought you stopped yelling."

"It's Christmas I deserve one more time to yell! Shut up and keep folding!"

"Don't you think the name *Helen and Lilly's Cranes* sounds like a good business?"

"No! Fold! Fold, wish, and shut up!"

"Oh."

"Yeah. Oh."

Christmas night came and when Lilly slept, her finger bones aching from folding so many birds, she dreamt of taking ordinary paper, crumbling it up into a ball and when she opened her hands a real bird would be released into the air flying from her palms each time. Each time that real bird would take a shit on the bald spot of her son-in-law's head. It was the best dream she could dream up at the time.

They say that being active makes you younger. The local martial arts academy sent a tai chi instructor to Bradley-Bell. Out of the 75 seniors only 13 showed for the class. Craig Ho was the instructor but he went by the name Crane Master Craig the Bionic Chinaman, a name he gave himself. He was an amputee; his right leg was a metal prosthetic. He could kick with it, crouch low, and run, he made Lilly's degenerative arthritis look like a scrape or a bruise. Helen was intrigued. It was the only day she didn't fold. Lilly sat in the wheel chair and watched the thirteen seniors attempt to do Tai Chi. It looked like a bunch of slow Chinese line-dancing to her. "You can join us if you'd like," The Bionic Chinaman said. "We have Tai Chi for wheel chair users, too. Just look at me. Nothing is impossible. Nothing is." Lilly did the hand movements. The breathing was the important thing. There was to be Tai Chi in the garden every Tuesday and Thursday free of charge.

It would be on the eve prior to New Years Eve that Sydney would visit her mother for the last time. She found her mother in her room doing the thing that gave her the most meaning. What she had become was a folder of birds. A creaser of cranes. "Mom! Your room!" There was only one walk way. A trail wide enough for Lilly to use her walker to get from the door where her wheel chair was parked, to her work desk which sat adjacent to her bed and a trail way that led to her bathroom—which if she were to start wearing diapers she wouldn't need to use that much—she could keep folding and not have to ever use the toilet. Cranes were her life. Cranes covered the floor outside the boundaries of the walk way. She hung cranes from her ceiling by strings. Suspended from above, the surrealist marionettes they were. The window was covered with cranes taped to the glass. She could no longer look out to see the garden. Cranes were on the toilet, inside the medicine cabinet, on the counter. She slept under them, she slept above them. Cranes were on the floor under her bed. White ones, red ones, pink ones, yellow ones, aquamarine ones, pastels, mauve cranes, fuchsia birds, birds of multiple paper feathers. "Mom! Your room!" was all that Sydney could say. Cranes taped to the television screen, cranes taped to the radio, cold cranes inside the refrigerator, on top of the refrigerator, magnets moved aside for the cranes that were taped to the outside of the refrigerator.

The warning signs of dementia are social withdrawal, memory loss, repeating the same words, mood swings, but it wasn't dementia that moved Lilly to live among the birds.

"Mom! Your room!"

"Come on in. Have a seat."

"Where?"

"Anywhere. Just move things over." She didn't look at her daughter, she just kept folding.

"What are you doing, mom?"

"Folding paper cranes."

"I can see that, but *what* are you doing?"

"*Folding* paper cranes like I said."

"I know. I—*WHY*, mom, why are you folding *this* many cranes? And you haven't even open the other Christmas gifts we sent you."

"I'll get to them. Eventually. Don't rush me. I'm an old lady."

"Mom, are you feeling okay?"

"Never felt more chipper, dear. Never felt more chipper." Lilly finished her crane and tossed it over her shoulder. In the spiritual world the bird actually flew. In the world of flesh and gravity the paper landed on the floor behind her. She reached for another sheet to fold.

"Mom."

"Daughter."

"Mom! Look at me! You're not looking at me!"

"I'm busy."

"Mom!" Sydney yelled.

"Daughter!" Lilly yelled back.

"I don't want you to do this anymore."

"Do what?"

"Do this, mom. *This*—this is insane. You can't even walk in here!"

"Has it occurred to you that I can't even walk *out there*?"

"Mom."

"Why do you keep calling me that?"

"Calling you what?"

"That word 'mom'. Why?"

"You're not making any sense."

"What does anymore? What does?"

"What?" Sydney's face flushed with tears. "Mom. I just want the best for you."

Lilly finished folding the crane and threw it at her daughter's face. "Get out!"

"Mom?"

"Get out!" she screamed.

"Mom?"

"Get out of my nest!"

"Mom?!"

"Get out!"

Sydney left startled stepping on the cranes that were on the floor.

Fake world. Selfish scared coward world. Just let me die. Maybe I'm selfish to say this but just let me die. Somebody dies at least once a season here. Four seasons in one year and someone dies at least once a season here. I hate it here. I will walk again...I will walk again...I will walk again...I will walk again...I will walk again...I will walk.

It would be the eve of New Years the final day of the dying year that Helen Nakamura would finish 999 cranes. Her wish was to leave Bradley-Bell. Where? She had no plan. She just knew she would leave. While

Lilly folded in the garden in her wheel chair, Helen did what little Tai Chi moves she remembered.

"Do you believe in God?" Lilly asked.

"No," Helen retorted. "I believe in cranes. Keep folding. You talk too much."

"I used to believe in God when I was a girl. That was a long time ago. I married an atheist. My husband used to say that the only god he believed in was his dog. Because dog is god spelled backwards or something like that. How come you never talk about your husband, was he good to you?"

"He's dead. What good is he to me dead? What more is there to talk about? Keep folding." Helen raised her arms and gracefully elongated them in a tai chi posture called crane spreads wings.

"I know I wasn't the best mother in world I made mistakes. I wouldn't let Sydney join the girl scouts when she wanted to. I sheltered her. I laughed at her when she wanted to go to college. I was mean to all of her boyfriends. I wouldn't let her go on school trips, I just wanted her to be safe that's all. All those child abductions that were going on. I kept her at home for that reason. I thought I was doing a good job. I thought. This is maybe how she pays me back. Maybe this is her revenge. Sticking me in this retirement home. I didn't used to believe in God because of the suffering I would see around me. If God existed, how could there be so much suffering? I think now all of this suffering is making me believe in God. Suffering is so tailor made. So precise. So ordered. There has to be a God or a Devil or something—none of this pain is random. Maybe God does exist; He's just a bad mom like me."

"Keep folding. I don't want to hear philosophy."

"Why aren't you folding today?"

"Because I'm done. Kaput. Kapooie."

"Kaput?!"

"I finished my 999. I want to save my one last crane for the first day of the New Year."

"Oh."

"Yeah. Oh."

"May I ask a favor of you?"

"No. Shut up and fold."

"I would like to be with you when you fold your last crane. I want to be there to see if the wish comes true."

"You sound like a lesbian to me now! No! I don't want a woman to be in my room at night when I fold my last crane!"

"No, Helen."

"Why? Why do you want to watch me fold my final crane?"

"Because I'm beginning to believe."

"Believe on your own. Keep folding. I'm doing tai chi."

Later that night the young at heart gathered in the lobby to watch the Times Square ball drop; the old at heart were nestled snug in their beds. Lilly and Helen went to the garden not to fold but to get away from the New Years racket. Helen rolled Lilly to the grass until the wheel chair could no longer budge. Lilly rose from her seat, her trembling legs held her back from walking even a moderate pace. She held onto Helen's shoulder grimacing at every step. The arthritis shot from her knees down through her shins and to her ankles. It then shot all the way up to her hips. It even gave her migraines. Her teeth chattered from the pain. Merely walking to the center of the lawn was a battle. Helen held the watch, Lilly held the silver pistol; the gift her husband gave her for their 40th wedding anniversary years ago when he was still alive. The throbbing in her knees caused her trigger hand to shake. "Don't point it at me!" Helen urged. Lilly gripped the gun with both hands. She held it above her head looking up at the moon. "You have two minutes to go. Don't shoot yet," Helen warned. Lilly's hands trembled. Facing the sky gave her a headache. "Okay one minute. Get ready." Lilly's arms were tired. She lowered the gun. "No! Don't point it at me!" She raised the gun back up, aiming at the big dipper. The moon was too pretty to shoot. "Nine, eight, seven, six—I hope it doesn't back fire—four, three two, one. Happy New Year!"

Shot one was for the past.
Shot two was for the present.
Shot three was for the future.
Shot four was for the pain of living.
Shot five was for a painless afterlife.
Shot six was for hope.

Lilly missed the big dipper, and shot the moon instead.

He wrote with tears. Every poem. He wrote with his eyes closed, and that was how Helen learned to fold cranes blindfolded. He believed that every poem should be wept out before it was written out. And he wrote her one thousand paper poems in two and one half years. And every day she rejected him. They met at work. She worked at a desk. He was the delivery guy. Delivering mail and packages to her boss. With every package or letter, he'd also send Helen a new poem. Short. Maybe five lines, maybe three lines. At most eight. But he wrote every one with his eyes closed. Thinking of no one but her. Once a week he'd ask her out on a date. To lunch. Every time she'd say no. Dinner? No. Movie?

No. He'd offer to cook. No. She took his poems and he took her nos in return. He told her he loved her after the five hundred eighty sixth poem. With it he sent a special note. And attached was a key. A silver one. The note said. "The key to Harry's heart". She never was annoyed. Or suspicious. But she smiled after every poem she read. She would read them on her lunch break or at night before she went to bed. She smiled when she refused his offers to date. Her eyes changed after the five hundred eighty sixth poem. By the seven hundredth poem, it was as if they communicated telepathically. Harry stopped asking her out. He would deliver boxes to her boss. Stop by her desk, hand her a poem and leave. This happened for two hundred poems. By the time of the nine hundredth poem, she finally touched his hand. Finally. Never once did they date. Never once did they see a movie together or drink coffee or go to a restaurant. There were no deep conversations other than the words of Harry's poems and the look in Helen's eyes the day after she read them. And every day was a "day after" because every day was a new poem. Harry knew she loved him by the nine hundredth and seventieth poem. He knew he would marry her and she did too. Love is stupid. Love is senseless. By the nine hundred and ninety ninth poem he would propose. She knew it was coming. She wore fuchsia that day. She wore that color because it was in 300 of his 1000 poems. She looked beautiful in it. No movies, no coffee, no long walks through parks, no jewelry, no sex, no kisses, no hugs, just 1000 poems. She saved every one. The day he delivered his one thousandth poem, she finally agreed to have lunch with him though he didn't ask. She took him by the hand and they left the office. They went to the court house across the street and they got married. Helen Hatori became Helen Nakamura. They told no one and went back to work. After work they went to the airport and flew to Hawaii for a honeymoon. They called in sick numerous times. No one asked. No one cared. Sometimes love is magical that way. There was no ring. There was no fling. 1000 pieces of paper only. Lines of words. Each one written by hand, blue ink on white. It was when they were married and they laid in bed after the first night they made love that Harry told Helen how he wrote his poems. How he would sit at a table shut his eyes and perfectly and patiently write each letter as if it were calligraphy. He shut his eyes because there was a meditation involved. Poem was equal to prayer. Helen believed him. He was a good husband.

And then God took him away.

Or borrowed him.

When he died, Helen did not cry, she yelled. She yelled because she loved every fragment of him. She could no longer speak to people she had to yell. She yelled at Lilly, she yelled at herself, she yelled at God, she yelled at the trees. It wasn't because she was old and cruel. It was only because the man that wrote her one thousand paper poems perfectly was taken away from her. Maybe if she yelled every time, he could hear her in the afterlife. Maybe if she spoke in this life a little louder he'd hear her from the next life. Love is stupid. Love is strange that way. Love is magical.

He who loses his dreaming is lost.

Though Helen slept the night she folded her 1000th crane, though she was cozy and snug under a blanket, she was wide awake. She was in the garden doing tai chi, spreading her arms like a crane and stepping perfectly. It began to rain. But it was not a cold rain. Out of that rain returned Harry. Holding his one thousandth and one poem. Harry was a good husband. Love is stupid. It is magical. It is senseless. It is ageless. And it matters as much as rain in a garden matters. When she took the one thousandth and one piece of paper from Harry, she no longer needed to sleep in her bed. She no longer needed to breathe the air of this life, this petty existence. This feeble world. She no longer needed to be alone. She no longer needed to be old. She no longer needed to be in a retirement home. She no longer needed to fold any more cranes. She no longer needed to yell every time she spoke. She, too, was senseless, magical, timeless. She, too, was as rain was in a garden. God may have taken Harry from her or borrowed him, but the moment she accepted his one thousandth and one poem, she took Harry back. Helen borrowed Harry back from God forever. **You may have created him. You may have given him life. But he is mine! Great Creator, he is mine!** And once again they were each others.

Morning came. The first day of the New Year. Everyone in Bradley-Bell woke up to the world except Helen.

When someone dies in a retirement home there is a long silence. Even the Alzheimer's patients know something has changed.

When Helen died, Lilly didn't eat for two days. She didn't fold for five days. Her soul was silenced. She stopped listening to music. She stopped speaking to the others. On the sixth day when she began folding again, she was finally able to shut her eyes and fold a crane perfectly. Blinded from the colors and shapes of her environment. That magical thing that Helen had—being able to fold blindfolded—was no longer magical; but masterable. To the novice, to the spectator it was spectacular but it was nothing to Lilly. Eyes open, eyes closed, a crane was a crane, a wish was a wish. *He who loses his dreaming is lost.*

People forget that retirement homes are haunted places. Ghosts walk throughout the halls. Ghosts visit the rooms. Ghosts moan at night, but the old are too hard of hearing to know this. Some of them are so forgetful that it doesn't matter to them that they are there. Spirits go unnoticed, unfeared.

They kept Helen Nakamura's room vacant for two months and then moved a newcomer in. Eventually that newcomer would die and be replaced by another and then another but Lilly didn't want to stay to see that happen. She folded cranes until she lost count of how many she had folded. She could have had 1000, she could have had 1070. She didn't know, nor cared to know anymore. She folded until her fingers bled and her knees no longer ached. And that was her cue. When her knees no longer ached. She rose from her wheel chair emotionless as if in a trance. It was her wish to walk again without the help of a walker or someone else. Perhaps the ghost of Helen Nakamura was helping her walk but at least it looked as though she walked on her own. She left her room. She left the lobby. She left for the side walk and down to the street corner. The air smells different when you are free. She shut her eyes to hear birds. Different birds that don't hang around old peoples' homes. When the light told her to cross, she opened her eyes and stepped forward.

For many reasons life is unreasonable.

A crowd of people made a circle around the scene.

Some dumb driver hit her in the cross walk. He had too much to drink.

"Any of a number of lilies with long, narrow leaves and bright flowers that usually last only a day" is how Webster defines the day lily.

For many reasons life is not reasonable. But Lilly walked. Finally.

Some see a white light when they die.

Some are able to watch their entire life without commercials.

Some see the Creator. Some see the Death Angel.

Some see nothing at all.

Lilly saw cranes.

Authors

William Cass has had over 200 short stories accepted for publication in a variety of literary magazines such as *J Journal*, *december*, *Briar Cliff Review*, and *Zone 3*. He has received three Pushcart nominations and won writing contests at Terrain.org and *The Examined Life Journal*. He lives in San Diego, California.

Jerry Cunningham writes short stories - mainly humorous - and often based on folktales and myths from around the world. His main influences are Bernard Malamud, Isaac Bashevis Singer and Gabriel Garcia Marquez. Jerry has also published two historical works. He's a grandfather with a white beard and lives in Portland, Oregon.

Larry Handy leads the award-winning poetry band Totem Maples. His fiction, nonfiction, and poetry appear in such journals as *Cog*, *Proximity*, *Quiddity*, *Rivet*, *Straight Forward Poetry* and elsewhere. He holds an MFA from the University of California, Riverside. His essay "What to Do When Grandma Has Dementia" was nominated for a Pushcart Prize. When not writing he is practicing Chinese martial arts or running 26.2 mile marathons. SoCal is his home.

Scott Pedersen is a writer based in Wisconsin. His work has appeared in *Falling Star Magazine*, *Louisiana Literature*, *The MacGuffin*, *In Parentheses* and anthologies from *Propertius Press*. When not writing fiction, he enjoys performing in a traditional Celtic band.

Kevin Stadt holds a master's degree in teaching writing and a doctorate in American literature; he currently teaches writing at Hanyang University. His fiction has appeared or is forthcoming in *Dark Fire Fiction*, *Enter the Aftermath*, *Kzine*, *Lazarus Risen*, *Outposts of Beyond*, *Phantaxis*, *Spring into SciFi*, *Stupefying Stories*, *Utopia Science Fiction*, and many more. He lives in South Korea with his wife and sons, who are interdimensional cyborg pirates wanted in a dozen star systems.

Thank you to the Wapshott Press sponsors, supporters, and Friends of the Wapshott Press.

Muna Deriane
Kit Ramage
Rachel Livingston
Laurel Sutton
Thomas Loper
Kathleen Warner
Ann and John Brantingham
David Meischen
John O'Kane
Suzanne Siegel
Toni Rodriguez
LindaAnn LoSchiavo
James and Rebecca White
Robert Earle and Mary Azoy
Steve Misuraca
Alice Frances Wickham
James Wilson
Phil Temples
Richard Whittaker
Ann Siemens
Kathy Bonagofsky

The Wapshott Press is a 501(c)(3) not-for-profit press publishing work by emerging and established authors and artists. We publish books that should be published. We are very grateful to the people who believe in our plans and goals, as well as our hopes and dreams. Our website is at www.WapshottPress.org. Donations gratefully accepted at www.Donate.WapshottPress.org.

www.ingramcontent.com/pod-product-compliance
Lightning Source LLC
LaVergne TN
LVHW010106110826
845155LV00028B/517

* 9 7 8 1 9 4 2 0 0 7 3 9 5 *